Happy New Year MURDER

BonzaiMoon Books LLC
Houston, Texas
www.bonzaimoonbooks.com

This is a work of fiction. Names, characters, places and incidents either are the product of the authors' imaginations or are used fictitiously, and any resemblance to actual persons, living or dead, business establishments, events, or locales is entirely coincidental.

1

As the firecrackers shrieked up toward the indigo sky and exploded into sparkling, rainbow-colored starbursts, Roland "Beanie" Bean smiled as his boys, four-year-old Ethan, and two-year-old Evan, laughed, and squealed and clapped their hands.

"Did you see that, Daddy?" Ethan hopped up and down on the blanket spread out in the grass. "The firecrackers said pop, pop, pop, pop, pop, pop!"

"Fire crack pop!" Little Evan did a little dance on his chubby, wobbly legs. "Pop fire crack!"

Beanie glanced around. Several feet away, in all directions, friends and families huddled and congregated on the expansive, sloping lawn of the park in their modest, working-class neighborhood, Oyster Farms. Like himself, and his wife Noelle, many sat on lawn chairs and canvas stadium seats, clustered in circles. Tonight, residents gathered to celebrate at the annual New Year's Eve Festival, which technically wasn't a festival. There were no vendor booths, amusement rides, or petting zoo. But the atmosphere was festive. There was a good crowd, positive energy, island music, and a local food truck, hired by the Homeowner's Association.

The weather was pleasant, a typical balmy, ocean-scented tropical evening. But in addition to the laughter and conversation, there was a palpable excitement, a current of anticipation for the coming new year and the possibilities it might hold.

There was a feeling of reflection, as well, Beanie sensed, as his neighbors passed, saying hello, or offering a wave. A recollection of the previous year, remembering the triumphs and disappointments, the successes, and failures, the missteps, and milestones. Beyond the recollection was a reconciliation, a recounting of the good and the bad, which hopefully added up to more positive than negative. Finally, there was a reckoning. Problems to be dealt with, issues to leave behind, and promises to carry forward.

"Beanie, my friend!"

Recognizing the voice, floating somewhere behind him, Beanie gave his wife a look, which she returned, with a chuckle and shrug of her shoulders. With a resigned sigh, Beanie rose from the old, battered chair he'd found in the backyard shed, and faced Anthony Mendez, a neighbor who lived a few houses down on the same street as Beanie, Dolphin Lane.

As usual, the seventy-something, who reminded Beanie of the actor, George Hamilton, was tan and trim, dressed in his customary pastel colors. Tonight, he'd donned a peach-colored shirt, powder blue slacks, and pale-yellow deck shoes.

"Hey, how are you?" asked Beanie, greeting the man with a hearty handshake.

"Doing great!" Mendez smiled as he greeted Noelle and waved to the boys, who waved back with shouts of glee as more firecrackers exploded against the starry sky. "Wonderful night for firecrackers."

Nodding, Beanie agreed.

"Hey, I meant to tell you that you looked good on television," said Mendez, clapping Beanie on the shoulder.

Laughing, Beanie said, "It was all make-up and lighting. Trust me."

"But that story was crazy!" Mendez frowned and shook his head.

The story Mendez referred to, which had garnered Beanie national attention with fifteen-second guest spots on several morning news shows around the world, was more than crazy. It had been downright insane. Heinous. Evil. Frightening. What Beanie thought might be a routine investigation into a shooting at the Adagio Bay outdoor mall turned out to be a once-in-a-lifetime story.

The sad, sordid tale of Luther Tindall had riveted the world. But only for a few days. Beanie's virality had burned hot and bright but was ultimately short-lived. Soon, another sad, sordid saga took the place of Tindall's high crimes and malfeasance.

"Some of the things people try to get away with just astound me," said Mendez, shaking his head. "Just like our sick, twisted neighbor."

"Don't remind us," said Noelle, who Beanie realized had been listening to the conversation as she also kept a hawk-like watchful eye on the boys. "I don't want to think about that horrible man. Just saying his name feels like saying some curse that would conjure him up."

Not surprised by his wife's vehemence, Beanie chuckled. "Tell us how you really feel, babe."

Mendez said, "I agree with you, Mrs. Bean. When I think that I lived a few houses away from that nutcase, I shudder. I went to his house. He had coffee with me at my place. And all the time, I was entertaining a cold-blooded psychopath!"

"Well, I don't know how any of us could have known the kind of person he was," said Beanie, keeping his tone non-committal, hoping to move away from the subject of the psycho who lived down the street. His reluctance to speak on the topic had to do with inner conflict regarding his investigative skills. He considered himself a reporter with sharp deductive and inductive skills, proficient at going beyond suspicions and speculation to uncover the truth. He'd believed himself to be a good judge of character, able to discern lies, half-truths, gaslighting, and other forms of deception. And yet, he hadn't been able to realize he'd trusted the wrong person. A sly, cunning man who'd almost killed him. There had been clues he'd missed. Red flags he'd inadvertently ignored. Missed clues that could have cost him his life. Could have made Noelle a young widow and his boys fatherless. The thoughts sobered Beanie. Made him question his judgment and investigative acumen.

"So, what big case are you working on now?" asked Mendez, the very definition of a nosy, gossipy neighbor, who possessed a state-of-the-art security surveillance system, far too sophisticated for his modest abode. And yet, Mendez's security had helped Beanie catch their neighborhood killer.

"Nothing big, at all," said Beanie.

"Thank goodness," remarked Noelle, giving her two cents. "I keep telling Roland to stop becoming part of the story. Investigate the story and write the story like other journalists. But, no. Beanie has to always put himself in a position to get himself killed."

"Not always," said Beanie, trying to mitigate his wife's concerns, which he knew were valid. For some reason, he wasn't quite sure and hadn't spent too much time ruminating about it, he generally found himself in the crosshairs of a killer. He wasn't quite sure when his career had become so dangerous, but he suspected it had begun when—

Raucous cheers and whistles broke out as more firecrackers streamed into the air.

"Nice of Moreaux to spring for the fireworks," remarked Mendez.

Beanie nodded. Kenneth Moreaux, a local businessman who owned several houses in the neighborhood which he operated as rental properties, was known for his philanthropy. Born in Little Turkey, the impoverished enclave near St. Killian International Airport, Moreaux had made it his mission to do good works across the island.

"Especially since he probably can't afford the expense," said Mendez.

"What do you mean?" asked Beanie.

"Since he lost his stake in Island Quik Loans," said Mendez, "I heard he's had some financial troubles."

"I wasn't aware of that," said Beanie. He knew Moreaux no longer owned an interest in the payday and title loan business he'd co-founded with his childhood friend, Saul Biaggio, but he'd thought Moreaux had started an automobile insurance company to supplement his rental home income.

"It's a shame," said Mendez, shaking his head. "Moreaux is a good guy. Biaggio did him dirty. Tricked him. Stole the company from him."

"Interesting," said Beanie. He recalled his colleague, Caleb Olivier, writing a few articles about Saul Biaggio, the principal owner of Island

Quik Loans, but he didn't know the details. As a crime reporter, he rarely paid attention to the business section of the paper.

"Biaggio claims to care about the community, but he's a snake," said Mendez. "He kicked Moreaux when he was down."

"How so?"

Mendez said, "After Moreaux's accident, he was in a bad way. Instead of supporting Moreaux, Saul forced Moreaux out of the company. Said Moreaux's injuries were hindering his ability to make good business decisions."

Beanie did remember hearing neighborhood gossip about Moreaux's traumatic brain injury. After crashing his car into a tree during a tropical storm, the man suffered brain swelling. Moreaux recovered, but some residents claimed Moreaux was different. That he didn't act the same. There was talk of wild, violent mood swings and forgetfulness.

Having never met Moreaux, Beanie couldn't confirm or deny any personality or behavioral differences. But if Moreaux had exhibited any type of cognitive impairment, then Saul Biaggio probably felt justified in getting rid of Moreaux, despite appearing callous and cutthroat.

Glancing at his watch, Mendez said, "Listen, it was great to see you and your family. I'm going to see if I can find Wanda Barnes."

"Wanda Barnes?" Beanie frowned, recalling the widow, a buxom, 1950's pinup model lookalike, who still resided on Dolphin Lane, despite living in a house that had seen much tragedy.

With a leering grin, Mendez waggled his eyebrows and said, "She might need someone to kiss when the clock strikes twelve."

As Mendez strode away, meandering through the crowd, Noelle stood and shook her head.

"Does that old goat really think Wanda Barnes would be interested in him?" asked Noelle.

Shrugging, Beanie said, "If he thinks he has a chance with a woman half his age, who am I to burst his bubble? I'm just glad that I have someone to kiss at midnight."

Smiling, Noelle slipped into his embrace. "Yes, you do ... "

2

Midnight had come and gone five hours ago.

It was a new year, though Beanie hardly noticed, and didn't feel very different.

At the park, three hours *before* the clock struck twelve, the boys started to get tired and cranky, so he and Noelle packed up their blankets and chairs and decided to call it a night. At home, after their baths, the boys watched more fireworks from the living room window, then went to bed at ten. With the kids tucked in, Beanie and Noelle talked and reminisced until midnight, where they shared a kiss to usher in the next three hundred and sixty-five days.At present, Beanie was wrestling with the key to the shed in their backyard, trying to insert it into the lock.

After they'd put the boys to bed, Noelle enticed him by suggesting a glass of champagne, which Beanie thought was a great idea. Beanie had planned to return the old lawn chairs to the shed, but after the bubbly, he found himself not in the mood.

For some reason, Beanie had woken up a little before five in the morning. Finding himself unable to get back to sleep, Beanie thought about the lawn chairs. Since he didn't want to toss and turn for another two hours, he decided to return the chairs to the shed, hoping the task might tire him out.

As Beanie peered at the lock, trying to see in the dim pre-dawn gloom of the backyard, which was barely illuminated by strings of party bulbs around the perimeter of the patio, he wondered if it might be best to work from home and allow the boys to sleep in. Ethan would miss a day of pre-school and Evan would forgo time at the early childhood development center, but how productive would they be on less than the ten hours of sleep they normally got?

Bending closer to the lock, Beanie squinted, focusing on the keyhole.

As he'd told Mendez, Beanie wasn't working on any breaking news stories. For the past few weeks, since the Luther Tindall story broke, he'd been filing reports on run-of-the-mill, par-for-the-course crime, and malice. A few shootings in Hedwig Gardens, a rough, disenfranchised enclave of marginalized poor islanders, wouldn't really trend on social media, let alone break the internet.

Inserting the key into the hole, Beanie turned it and opened the lock, unclasping the U-shaped metal bar looped around the hasp. Swinging the door open, confronted with gaping darkness, Beanie paused. His heart rate increased. He wasn't afraid to go into the shed, so he wasn't sure about the sudden apprehension that washed over him. Although, he had several reasons for avoiding sheds. First, he'd nearly died in one. Second, years ago, a killer had broken into the backyard shed, and—

A brittle snap startled Beanie from his reverie.

Heart thudding faster, he leaned forward, trying to see through the darkness into the shed. What had made that sound? Had it come from inside the shed? Maybe a lizard, small mouse, or some other nocturnal creature had slipped through a crack. Standing still, Beanie listened. Nothing but normal neighborhood sounds. The wind rustled trees. Insects buzzed and chirped. Maybe he'd imagined it. Or maybe—

More snapping, mixed with a muted crashing, sent Beanie's blood pressure through the roof.

The sounds had come from behind the shed, near the back fence. For a second, he froze. Could be a larger animal. Possibly a goat. The breaking sound continued, making him wonder if something might be caught in the mature hibiscus trees lined along the fence. Maybe a cat?

Swallowing, Beanie took several cautious steps toward the side of the shed.

Peeking around the corner of the structure, he stared at the petals of the hibiscus bushes, which had grown to chest height since he'd planted them a few years ago. The leaves of the hibiscus swayed slightly, but he couldn't tell if some animal was trapped in the branches.

As his eyes had adjusted to the darkness, he was spatially aware of his surroundings. Wouldn't be a problem to walk the ten or so feet to the fence. He would probably determine that a large lizard was slithering through the bushes. He puffed his cheeks, then slowly let out the air. Why hadn't he just waited until daybreak to put the chairs back into the shed? And why was he hesitating now? Just find out what was in the bushes. Probably nothing.

Beanie took a step forward. And then another. Seconds later, he was standing in front of the bush, listening for sounds, looking for lizards, feeling like an idiot. He didn't see anything and hadn't expected to. For a moment, he stood still and listened again. Very faint music, maybe coming from a few streets away. Revelers keeping the party going, intent on dancing in the new year. A car driving, tires gliding over concrete. And more insects. More gently rustling leaves. Thankfully, no guns. The Palmchat Islands had laws against discharging firearms during celebratory activities. But that hadn't stopped people from shooting into the sky on New Year's Eve.

Anxious to put the chairs back into the shed and head inside, Beanie turned from the bushes.

Several feet away, a man rushed toward him.

3

Beanie froze, trying to think, to come up with a plan of action, to stay alive.

He longed for a shovel or a bat or any type of blunt object.

The man lurched closer, a shadowy figure in the darkness, a silhouette against the dim patio lights.

Thoughts bombarded his brain, swirling and swarming, flooding his mind with grim thoughts. He was about to be attacked. Robbed and killed. Beaten to within an inch of his life. And yet, he wouldn't go down without a fight. He would defend himself against whatever onslaught the man planned to bring. He had to think of Noelle and the boys. If this guy took him out, who would protect his family?

Beanie chose to go on the offensive, trying to get the upper hand. He started to swing, hoping to catch the guy in the jaw and put him off guard, but the man stumbled to the right and dropped to one knee in the grass.

Confused, Beanie took a step back. What was going on? Was the man inebriated? Had he stumbled away from a party, sloppy drunk and disoriented? Maybe he'd somehow wandered into the wrong backyard? Or maybe—

The man staggered to his feet, swaying.

"Who are you?" Beanie demanded, clinching his fists, ready to strike, if necessary. "What are you doing out here?"

Gasping, the man moaned and wobbled to the left, nearly tripping over his feet.

"Get out of my yard," Beanie ordered, figuring the guy was drunk, and not much of a threat. From the way the guy bobbed and weaved, he didn't seem coordinated or coherent. Beanie prayed he wouldn't puke all over the grass, which he'd cut a day ago, and contemplated calling the police.

The man lunged at him.

"Get back!" Beanie raised his fist. "Come near me and—"

"Help …" rasped the man, his voice a gravelly whisper. "Please … help …"

Shocked, Beanie lowered his arm. "What?"

"Please … help …" Moaning, the man dropped to his knees and toppled over onto the yard.

Though he wondered if the man might be faking an injury to trick him, Beanie nevertheless hurried to the guy and took a knee next to him. "What's the matter? Are you hurt?"

Eyes wide, the whites almost glowing in the darkness, the man expelled ragged breaths. "… me …"

Straining to hear what the man was saying, Beanie bent over him. "What did you say? Are you hurt? Should I call an ambulance?"

"… me … stabbed …"

A chill passed through Beanie. "Someone stabbed you?"

"Tammy …" the man rasped, then coughed. "Tammy … stabbed …"

"Where were you stabbed?" asked Beanie, then shook his head. "No, just … don't try to talk, okay? I'm going to—"

"Stabbed me …" The man groaned again. "Tammy …"

Though he wondered who Tammy was, and if the man was trying to tell him that someone named Tammy had stabbed him, Beanie didn't have time to interrogate the man. Or examine any wounds. He needed to call 911 before—

"Roland, what are you doing?"

Noelle's worried voice arrested Beanie for a moment. He glanced up and saw his wife jogging toward him.

"Elle, babe, go into the house and—"

"Oh my God!" Noelle stopped inches away from the collapsed man. "Who is that? What happened?"

"I'm not sure," said Beanie, looking up at his wife. "I think he's been stabbed."

"Stabbed?" Noelle shook her head. "What? How? Oh my God!"

"Babe, please go call 911," instructed Beanie, his nerves too frazzled for Noelle's histrionics. "I'm not sure how bad he's hurt, but we need to get an ambulance here now!"

<hr>

Twenty minutes later, the backyard, flooded with portable spotlights, swarmed with cops and EMS paramedics.

After finally convincing his wife to go into the house and call the police, Beanie stayed with the injured man, figuring out, from his examination and from the man's breathless whispers, that the guy had been knifed in the chest. Trying to staunch the flow of blood, Beanie had pressed his hand against the wound and encouraged the man to stop speaking. Although, he hadn't said anything other than what he'd first said. He kept whispering that he'd been stabbed and speaking the name Tammy.

Beanie hadn't been able to put anything about the wild incident together.

Relief flooded him when the paramedics and police barreled into the backyard, pushing him aside.

Now he was standing on his patio, Noelle next to him, giving a statement to Detective Philippi Janvier of the St. Killian Police Department. A gaunt, relatively tall Frenchman, Janvier was dressed in a linen suit with more wrinkles than an elephant and sported his usual smug sneer.

Beanie could hardly stand the detective, and that was an understatement. His ire toward the Frenchman began a few years ago when Janvier arrested Noelle for a murder she hadn't committed. To add insult to injury, when confronted with evidence that exonerated Noelle as a suspect, Janvier refused to consider the information. Relying on his own confirmation bias, Janvier could not conceive that he was wrong about Noelle. His inaction and ineptitude, in Beanie's opinion, had allowed a heartless killer to take the lives of two additional victims. When the murderer was finally apprehended, no thanks to Janvier, the man made no effort to right wrongs by admitting his failings. Grudgingly, he dropped his investigation against Noelle. To this day, the man had never apologized for his blunders.

"Reporter Bean," began Janvier, scowling. "What do you have to tell me about the events that transpired tonight?"

Beanie took a breath. Next to him, he could feel the rage emanating from Noelle, who held only ill will for the man who'd tried to destroy her life with circumstantial evidence. If he could get away with it, Beanie would have refused to talk to Janvier. But he was the detective assigned to the case, so Beanie would find a way to tolerate the man's suspicious, snarky attitude.

"Roland already gave his statement to the first responding officers," snapped Noelle, arms crossed as she glared at Janvier.

"I am sure he has, Mrs. Bean," said Janvier. "However, I would like to hear the events myself. And I would advise you to stick around as I will have questions for you, as well."

As Noelle scoffed and shook her head, Beanie decided to answer the detective's questions as quickly as possible. Might as well get it over with since it couldn't be avoided.

"I was in my backyard when I heard a noise," started Beanie, cutting his gaze toward the crime scene techs near the shed. Dressed in all white, with coverings over their shoes and hair, they moved about the structure and walked along the fence, snapping photos, and collecting items they sealed into plastic bags.

"Why were you in your backyard at five in the morning?" demanded Janvier.

"Roland was putting some chairs back into the shed," said Noelle.

"Please, Mrs. Bean, I must insist that your husband answer my questions," the detective said. "I will have questions for you and you may speak at that time."

Fearing his wife would blow a gasket at Janvier's patronizing tone, Beanie hurried to say, "I was going to put the chairs back in the shed—"

"Why did you take the chairs from the shed?" asked Janvier, his gaze shrewd.

Beanie resisted the urge to roll his eyes. "My wife and I wanted to sit on them. We took our boys to the annual New Year's Eve firework celebration at the neighborhood park."

"And your boys will be able to corroborate that?" asked Janvier, eyes shifting left and right.

"You will not talk to my children," Noelle said.

"Pretty much our whole neighborhood saw us there," said Beanie.

"I will need the names of neighbors who can prove that you, your wife, and your children attended the celebration at the park," said Janvier. "Please continue."

For a moment, Beanie was flabbergasted by the detective's audacity but quickly reminded himself that Janvier didn't like him, either. The man took pains to irritate and annoy Beanie whenever he could.

"While I was returning the chairs to the shed," said Beanie, praying for no further idiotic interruptions. "I heard a noise which I initially thought was a small animal but turned out to be a man I'd never seen before."

Consulting his phone, Janvier said, "And according to the statement to Officer Smith, you first thought the man was drunk, but as it turned out, he had been stabbed."

"Correct," said Beanie. "He was staggering and stumbling before he collapsed. And that's when he told me he was stabbed."

"Reporter Bean," began Janvier, glancing at him. "Why do you have blood on your shirt?"

"Not because Roland stabbed the man who collapsed in our backyard," snipped Noelle.

"Mrs. Bean, I must insist that your husband answer my questions," said Janvier. "And furthermore, I will determine if Reporter Bean stabbed the man who collapsed in your backyard or not."

Again, eager to quell Noelle's temper, Beanie said, "I'm not sure but I'm thinking I got blood on me when I tried to apply pressure to the man's wound so he wouldn't bleed to death while we were waiting for the ambulance."

"Mrs. Bean, you should be happy," said Janvier. "You will get a chance to speak as I have a question for you now."

Noelle glared at Janvier.

The detective said, "And it was you, and not your husband, who called the police?"

"That's right," said Noelle. "I went into the backyard and I saw the man lying in the grass. Roland told me the man was hurt and to call an ambulance."

"Reporter Bean," began Janvier, glancing at his phone again. "You told Officer Smith that the man spoke to you before he collapsed, is that right?"

Beanie nodded. "He told me he was stabbed."

"Did he say who stabbed him?" asked the detective.

"No, but ..." Beanie hesitated.

"But?" prompted Janvier.

"The man mentioned the name Tammy," said Beanie. "He didn't specifically tell me that Tammy stabbed him. He just said the name Tammy. It was hard to understand what he was trying to say. He was losing a lot of blood and wasn't coherent."

The detective rubbed his chin. "And did you ask who Tammy was?"

"I think I did," said Beanie. "But he didn't tell me."

"Hmmm ..." The detective narrowed his eyes. "Well, I suppose those are all the questions I have for now however, I do reserve the right to question you again, should I determine that you and your wife concocted this ridiculous story to cover up the fact that you murdered a man in cold blood."

After Janvier pivoted and headed across the yard toward the crime scene techs, Beanie chuckled and glanced at Noelle. "Can you believe that guy?"

"Yeah, actually, I can believe him," said Noelle, worry marring her lovely face. "What I can't believe is that, once again, somehow, you're part of the story that you're going to write …"

"What do you mean?"

"I mean a man bleeding to death finds his way into our backyard at the moment when you're putting away chairs in the shed, then collapses before telling you that he was stabbed and giving you the name Tammy, who may or may not have stabbed him, who knows?"

"Well, yeah, but … " Beanie sighed. "Elle. Come on. It's not like I knew the guy was going to collapse in our backyard while I was putting chairs back into the shed."

"I know that, but …"

"But?"

"But you could have put the chairs in the shed last night," said Noelle.

"And if I had, then I would have likely found a dead man in our backyard in the morning," pointed out Beanie. "That would have been worse."

Pinching the bridge of her nose, Noelle said, "You're right. And I'm being irrational right now. It's not like you planned this or anything."

Beanie scoffed. "I'm sure that's what Janvier thinks."

Noelle walked into his outstretched arms and rested her head on his chest. "I'm just worried, Roland. Just seems like every time you're part of the story, you end up in a life-or-death situation."

"How about this," said Beanie, kissing the top of her head. "I'll talk to Vivian and ask her to let Stevie, or maybe even Caleb, cover the story. And then instead of being part of the story, I'll be a witness."

Noelle glanced up at him. "You think Vivian will go for that?"

Thinking of his editor, Vivian Thomas-Bronson, who prioritized compelling, gripping stories that trended and made an immediate impact, Beanie said, "Well, we'll see …"

4

"So, what did Viv say about you being the witness to the story instead of part of the story?" asked Stevie Bishop, one of Beanie's coworkers at the *Palmchat Gazette*, where they both worked as crime reporters.

At ten in the morning, he and Stevie were taking a quick break, sitting at a table in the corner of the breakroom, a large airy space with ceiling-to-floor windows that looked out toward a side street.

Beanie took a sip of his first cup of coffee of the morning. As he stifled another yawn, he knew he'd need another cup soon. The fact that he'd been able to drag himself to work after the early morning drama shocked him. "She was not exactly on board with that idea," said Beanie, recalling his conversation with the award-winning former foreign correspondent. Sitting across from the sun-kissed caramel beauty, Beanie wasn't surprised when Vivian pointed out to him that his stories were so popular and trended because he was a central part of them.

"That's becoming your brand," said Vivian. "People look forward to reading what you write because they get that personal eyewitness account. You have a real stake in the outcome of the story."

Beanie had rubbed his jaw. "Yeah, I guess."

"You don't have to guess," said Vivian. "I have the numbers to prove it. Readers were engaged in the egg hunt murder because your little boy found the dead body."

Shaking his head, Beanie said, "Don't remind Noelle about that."

"And they couldn't get enough of the story about the ex-pat who dropped dead while celebrating Thanksgiving," said Vivian.

Eric Barnes, Beanie had thought, remembering Mendez's attempt to flirt with the man's good-looking widow.

"And let's not forget your crazy neighbor who was obsessed with the Fury."

"Actually, let's forget about him," said Beanie.

But he'd understood Vivian's assessment. And he was becoming amenable to the idea of his brand as the reporter who was part of the story despite his wife's objections.

"So, you have to write the story," said Stevie.

"I have to write the story," confirmed Beanie, yawning. "And speaking of writing the story, Vivian wants an elaborate, detailed account so I need to call Fields."

"Got to get the detailed details," said Stevie, taking a sip of his bottled water.

Standing, Beanie frowned. "Detailed details?"

"Just something Sophie says," explained Stevie, grinning as he shook his head.

Thinking of Sophie Carter, the junior reporter who'd begun her career at the *Palmchat Gazette*'s St. Killian office but had been assigned a position at the paper's satellite location in St. Mateo, Beanie chuckled. "Figures she would say something like that. How's she doing? Have you heard from her?"

"Yeah, we try to keep in touch," said Stevie. "Mainly through texts. You know, she's got a cat."

"A cat?"

"A Calico named Callie," said Stevie, before his brows furrowed. "Although, actually, the cat isn't really her cat, she just knows the cat."

"Yeah, I'm sure she does," said Beanie, heading out of the breakroom, not particularly interested in his peculiar coworker.

Back at his tiny desk in his small cubicle, Beanie called Officer

Damon Fields, a trusted confidential source at the St. Killian police station. After working together for several years, his relationship with Fields had become congenial, and the two were now good friends.

"I'm sure I know why you're calling," said Fields.

Beanie sighed. "Guess you heard about the guy who collapsed in my backyard."

"I probably would have been there if I hadn't been called to a shooting in Handweg," said Fields. "Man, I have to be honest, I'm starting to worry about you."

"Worry about me?" asked Beanie, slightly confused as he turned to his computer and opened a Word document to take notes. "Why?"

"Everywhere you go, people drop dead!"

Picking up on the teasing in Field's tone, Beanie said, "You sound like Noelle. She's tired of me being part of the story. But, like I told her, I'm not out looking for dead bodies to trip over."

"But that's not what happens," said Fields. "You don't find dead people. You go places and people die."

Beanie frowned. "You know, when you put it like that …"

"I'm just joking with you," said Fields, chuckling. "But … it is kind of weird."

"Well, the guy who collapsed in my yard last night isn't dead," said Beanie. "At least, he was still alive when the paramedics wheeled him into the ambulance."

"As far as I know, which isn't much," began Fields, "he was taken to the hospital, where he had surgery, and was placed in ICU. So, yes, he's still alive."

"Thank God," said Beanie.

"For now …" added Fields.

"Was that necessary?" asked Beanie.

"Sorry," said Fields, his tone somewhat contrite. "Anyway, I don't have much info on the case."

"What about the name of the victim?" asked Beanie. "I didn't get it last night."

"Saul Biaggio," said Fields.

"Saul Biaggio?" echoed Beanie, shocked. "Are you serious?"

"Medical records and Biaggio's wife confirmed his identity following his surgery," said Fields.

"Wild," said Beanie, his fingers flying over the keyboard. His neighbor's assessment of Saul Biaggio came back to him. *Biaggio claims to care about the community, but he's a snake.* Had Mendez been spouting unjustified criticism? Or was Biaggio a wolf in sheep's clothing?

Beanie remembered a human-interest piece, written by his coworker Caleb Olivier, about Saul Biaggio donating money to a local youth cricket club. The funds had made it possible for the team, a talented group of kids from the marginalized Little Turkey neighborhood, to travel to Europe. With their room and board secured, the team competed in a tournament where they'd won third place.

Beanie wondered if Biaggio's good Samaritan act was a front for bad deeds. And, if so, had he been stabbed because of some malfeasant act he'd committed?

"Wild is right," agreed Fields.

"Any idea who stabbed him?" asked Beanie. "Or how he ended up in Oyster Farms? I seem to recall him being part of the Avalon Estates set."

"I have no idea how he ended up in Oyster Farms, but he and his wife were out on New Year's," said Fields. "They threw their annual New Year's Eve party at the Queen Palm Hotel."

"You think they were followed from the party?"

"That's what I think," said Fields. "Janvier thinks otherwise, not surprisingly."

Beanie scoffed. "Doesn't he always?"

Fields snorted. "Unfortunately."

"Well, I'll wait for you to get back to me," said Beanie.

"Actually …" Fields cleared his throat. "I might be able to get back to you tonight when you and Noelle join me and Amber for dinner. My place. Around seven? What do you say?"

Beanie paused. What he wanted to say was something that might upset his friend. Because what he wanted to say was that he didn't think Fields should be involved with Amber. Beanie's trepidation regarding Amber had nothing to do with the woman as a person. Amber was a good friend of Noelle's, and according to his wife, Amber was smart, kind, compassionate, and a great mother to her little girl, Ambrosia.

The problem with Amber was her father—Lime Shoes, a notorious PC-5 member who'd been active in the cartel, and its crooked, criminal dealings, for decades. What made the issue complicated was Beanie's relationship with the gangster. He and Lime Shoes had a perilous partnership. The old gang member was a confidential source, providing information about certain crimes, particularly malfeasance erroneously attributed to the cartel.

Upon their first meeting, Lime Shoes had explained that the cartel did not want Beanie accusing the PC-5 of crimes it hadn't committed. Thus, the old gangster would help Beanie get his stories right by sharing facts and details, especially when those facts and details exonerated the vicious island gang.

With Fields being a loyal, dedicated cop, committed to upholding the law, and Lime Shoes being a loyal gang member, committed to the PC-5, Beanie wasn't sure how Fields' relationship with Amber could work.

But, Beanie didn't voice his concerns.

Instead, he said, "Sounds great. I'll let Noelle know and we'll be there."

5

When Beanie and Noelle had arrived at Field's modest, modern apartment near the marina, they were greeted with gregarious frivolity by the officer and Amber, fetching in a pink sundress.

They'd indulged in Palmitos and casual conversation while Fields grilled goat kabobs on the patio and Amber made mashed plantains and peas in the kitchen. As the evening progressed, there was laughter, social commentary, good-natured ribbing, interesting confessions of misspent youth, ardent opinions regarding important issues of the day, gossip, and speculation about Ambrosia and Ethan, who alternately were sweet on and couldn't stand each other.

Now, as they lounged on the patio, relishing the balmy, lavender, and cinnamon-scented air, and watching the sky change from orange to pink to purple as the sun set, Noelle wanted to discuss Saul Biaggio.

Beanie felt he could have gone the rest of the night without introducing the subject, but he remembered Fields had promised him more information, and Vivian was eager for the story.

"You know what's crazy about Saul Biaggio showing up stabbed in our backyard?" asked Noelle.

Fields said, "No, what?"

Shaking her head, Noelle said, "Normally, Beanie will go somewhere and somebody will drop dead, but this time, the person dropped dead—"

"Actually, technically, Saul didn't drop dead. He's in a medically induced coma."

"That's right," said Amber.

"Okay, true," said Noelle, chuckling as she rolled her eyes.

Beanie continued, "And as for me going somewhere and someone dropping dead, that only happened once."

"No, it happened twice," corrected Noelle, giving him a triumphant look.

"Twice?" Amber laughed. "That's not enough times to declare a pattern."

"Thank you, Amber," said Beanie, raising his beer bottle to salute her.

"But it's twice too many," said Fields. "Once would be enough for me."

"Wait, you do know you're a cop, right?" Beanie frowned at his friend. "You're always going to be in a position to come across dead bodies."

"Yeah, but I mean, if I wasn't a cop," clarified Fields. "I would think it was a bit strange."

"No, I was wrong," announced Noelle, as though she'd had an eureka moment. "It happened three times."

"Three times?" Amber looked from Beanie to Noelle and then back to Beanie. "I don't know, Beanie. That might constitute a pattern."

"What were the three times?" challenged Beanie, staring at his wife, not sure he trusted her memory.

"Eric Barnes," began Noelle, holding up a finger. "The guy who lived in that beach shack. And your sister's ex-boyfriend. That's three."

"Is that right?" asked Fields.

"Yeah, that's right," muttered Beanie, taking another sip of beer.

"Told you!" crowed Noelle.

"Well, what I think is crazy is that Saul Biaggio ended up in your backyard," said Amber. "What was he doing in your neighborhood?"

"I agree," said Noelle. "He lives in Avalon Estates, right? That's quite far from Oyster Farms."

Beanie glanced at Fields. "You find out anything?"

"Not as much as I wanted to," said Fields, leaning back in his deck chair. "It was that kind of day. New year, new crimes, new altercations, new assaults, new robberies. But, I did learn that Janvier is suspicious of Biaggio's wife, Tammy Biaggio."

"Tammy?" Noelle gasped. "Are you serious?"

Beanie shared his wife's astonishment.

Fields looked confused. "Why wouldn't I be serious?"

"Did you read the statement I gave the first responders?" asked Beanie.

"Saul Biaggio told Beanie that Tammy stabbed him," said Noelle.

"What?" Amber's jaw dropped.

"Are you serious?" Fields asked Noelle.

Beanie said, "Wait, wait. I didn't tell Janvier that Biaggio told me Tammy stabbed him. I said that Biaggio said he was stabbed. And he said the name Tammy. But the man was disoriented and incoherent. He may have been speaking out of context."

"And he could have been telling you that his wife, Tammy, stabbed him," said Amber.

"Does Janvier think Biaggio's wife stabbed him?" asked Beanie.

"I'm not sure," said Fields. "Janvier went to speak with her this morning."

"And what did she tell Janvier?" asked Amber. "Did she confess to stabbing her husband? Did she try to kill him? Is she homicidal?"

Shaking his head, Fields said, "I don't know any details about the wife's conversation with Janvier."

Amber gaped at Fields. "Damon, you can't tell us that the wife talked to Janvier and then not tell us what the wife told him."

"Exactly," said Noelle.

Fields threw up his hands. "I can't tell you what Tammy Biaggio told Janvier because, as I already said, I don't know any details but if I did, trust me, I would tell you. But Janvier usually suspects the first person he interrogates, so I wouldn't be surprised if he thinks the wife did it."

Beanie shook his head. "And that's what bothers me. I'm reluctant to get behind Janvier's suspicions. The man has a knack for arresting the wrong person."

"True," agreed Noelle.

"How will you find out if Janvier is wrong about Tammy Biaggio, or not?" asked Amber.

"First, I need to talk to Tammy Biaggio," said Beanie.

"And what if she won't talk to you?" asked Amber.

Fields said, "I can probably get Beanie a copy of her statement."

"Well, I'd like a copy of that statement," said Amber, standing. "Because I swear, I have to know if she tried to kill her husband!"

Laughing, Noelle stood and began collecting the empty beer bottles. "I'll bet she didn't."

"Girl, that woman is from Avalon Estates," said Amber, gathering the empty plates. "You know how evil and crazy those rich people are! Remember, you told me what happened at that Easter egg hunt."

"Yeah, that was crazy," said Noelle, giggling as she and Amber announced they were going into the kitchen to clean up and would rejoin them with slices of mango cheesecake.

Once the women were out of earshot, Beanie leaned toward Fields. "Hey, let me ask you something. It's not about Biaggio."

Frowning, Fields asked, "What's it about?"

"Amber," said Beanie, before he had a chance to talk himself out of voicing his worries.

"What about Amber?"

"Actually, Amber's father," said Beanie, glancing toward the open patio doors. Several feet away, in the galley kitchen, his wife and her best friend laughed and talked as they tidied the dirty dishes. "Lime Shoes."

Fields' frown deepened as he let out a long exhale. "What about him?"

"Have you met him?"

"Not yet." Fields shook his head. "And I don't plan to ..."

"You don't plan to?" asked Beanie. "How are you going to manage that? He knows you're dating his daughter, right?"

"Yeah, I'm sure he does," said Fields, scratching his jaw as he glanced toward the kitchen. "But, what I meant was, I probably won't have to meet him."

Beanie was dubious. "You sure about that?"

Fields shrugged. "Amber and her father aren't close. She only talks to him because she wants Ambrosia to know her grandfather. There's no need for me to meet him."

Leaning back in his chair, Beanie sighed.

"What?" asked Fields.

Shaking his head, Beanie said nothing, wishing he'd kept his mouth closed.

"You think I'm making the wrong decision?" asked Fields, his voice lowered. "You think I need to meet the guy?"

"I think you need to prepare yourself for the possibility of meeting him," said Beanie.

"But how is that going to look?" asked Fields. "I'm a cop. He's PC-5."

"That's what you need to think about," said Beanie. "How will it look? What will your superiors think? How will your fellow officers feel? They know you're dating Amber?"

Fields shook his head. "I try to keep my personal life and professional life separate."

"Some of the higher-ups in the department might already know," said Beanie.

"Possibly, I'm not sure," said Fields. "Amber doesn't have the same last name as her father. She didn't grow up with him."

"I'm sure the island feds know Amber is Lime Shoe's daughter," said Beanie. "Other people are going to find out."

"Okay, if it becomes public knowledge—"

"When …" Beanie said.

Fields shrugged. "When it becomes public knowledge, I'll deal with it. Look Amber is not her father. Sins aren't visited on the children. No one is going to think anything about me dating her."

"I don't know about that," said Beanie.

"People don't think bad about you for marrying Noelle," said Fields, a hint of defiance in his tone. "And her father is Josue Chartres. Ruthless assassin. Carried out the cartel's Death List."

Beanie pinched the bridge of his nose. "Look, I just don't want to see you in a position where your loyalty to the force is questioned, or—"

"That's not going to happen, okay," said Fields. "Don't worry. And we gotta drop this conversation because Amber and Noelle are heading this way."

Nodding, Beanie held his peace as his wife and Amber walked out onto the patio carrying the mango cheesecake, small plates, and utensils.

6

Previously fortified by his second cup of coffee of the morning, Beanie strolled into the front entrance of St. Killian General Hospital, a soaring, spacious two-story vestibule where bright, natural light streamed through a wall of windows.

Half an hour ago, on his quest to get an interview with Saul Biaggio's wife Tammy, Beanie had done a public record search to find the businessman's address. As he expected, the Biaggios occupied a mega-mansion in Avalon Estates, the swanky, luxurious neighborhood featuring gigantic homes, palm-lined streets, and artful tropical landscaping.

The exclusive enclave also housed sinister secrets, a few Beanie had exposed during his investigations. As it turned out, there was just as much malice and mayhem among the rich as there was crime and poverty among the disadvantaged citizens of Handweg Gardens and Little Turkey.

Unfortunately, however, Tammy Biaggio wasn't home. According to the Biaggio's butler, a stern West Indian with a sour expression, Mrs. Biaggio was at the hospital visiting her husband. Beanie had thought about leaving his card but doubted the man would give it to his employer. Instead, he decided to waylay the wife at the hospital. A crass move, he figured, given she was probably frantic and worried, but Beanie was anxious to talk to her. Sure, he could have waited for Fields to forward him the police report but in his experience, the cops never provided any compelling details. Since many cops didn't like writing reports, they tended to focus on the facts. Most of the reports Beanie had read were all substance, no style.

Of course, soliciting an interview from Tammy Biaggio while she visited her husband was risky. She might refuse to talk to him. But Beanie figured that if she didn't want to speak to the media, it wouldn't matter where she was when he asked her to answer a few questions.

Moments later, at the semi-circular-shaped front desk, Beanie stopped to chat with the receptionist, a plump, gregarious fifty-something named Etta who went to his church. After stating his intentions—he was there to intercept a hospital visitor, hopefully, whose husband was in ICU—Beanie wished the receptionist a good day and headed to the elevators.

Inside, as the doors closed, he thought of the last time he'd come to the hospital to interview the loved one of a patient. Recalling that particular situation kept him from focusing on the times he'd ended up in the intensive care unit, fighting for his life.

Sometimes he wondered if his wife was right. Maybe being part of the story was too dangerous. Sure, his first-person accounts trended and could prove lucrative, but at what expense? He might get a podcast, or a book deal, or a spot as a correspondent on a true crime news show but was that worth risking his life?

The elevator doors opened, and Beanie walked out and headed to the nurse's station. There he inquired about Saul Biaggio, after introducing himself, and was refused any information about the man's condition. Beanie figured the nurse wouldn't be able to tell him anything. But when he asked if Mrs. Biaggio was with him, the nurse informed him that the wife was most likely in the waiting room, as the doctor was examining Biaggio at the moment.

Beanie thanked the nurse and then walked to the ICU waiting room.

The spacious area, with its soft blue walls, clusters of plush couches and chairs cordoned into L-shaped seating areas, palm trees, and large windows, was relaxing and peaceful, designed to soothe anxious visitors hoping for good news.

Scanning the waiting room, Beanie spotted the only occupant.

An elderly man slumped in a chair, snoozing, his chin lolling against his chest.

Disappointed, Beanie sighed. If Mrs. Biaggio wasn't in the ICU waiting room, then where could she be? He doubted the woman would have left the hospital. Had she gone to the ladies' room? Or maybe—

"You looking for Mrs. Biaggio?"

Glancing up, Beanie smiled and greeted the woman standing a few feet away. Dressed in pink scrubs, the friendly nurse's aide, Rhea Calais, fixed him with a dubious smirk. Rhea, who'd provided Beanie with information about a previous story, was an acquaintance whose mother-in-law was friends with Noelle's mom.

"One of the nurses told me she might be in the waiting room," said Beanie.

Rhea shook her head. "Mrs. Biaggio left about thirty minutes ago. She's been keeping a vigil for the last eight hours and needed to go home, shower, and get some rest before she comes back."

Beanie tempered his disappointment. "I was hoping to talk to her."

"You're not the only one," said Rhea.

"What do you mean?" asked Beanie, wondering if he had competition. St. Killian didn't have a local news station. Instead, the island relied on regional and international news organizations to stay abreast of current events. However, a few neighborhoods had small publications that focused on providing community news, current events and activities, and local government issues. Most neighborhood papers were run by a small staff—a publisher and one or two reporters. Saul Biaggio's attack was definitely worth reporting.

"Some scruffy guy in a leather jacket came to see Mrs. Biaggio," began Rhea, voice lowered as she leaned toward Beanie, her dark eyes alight with cautious concern. "He showed up when she was visiting her husband. We told him only family but he tells us he is family. So, we don't argue. He goes into the room and from what I saw, he didn't look like family."

"What did he look like?"

Rhea shook her head. "Bad news."

"Bad news?"

"And sounded like it, too."

Beanie frowned. "I don't understand."

"Well, first of all, he lied about being family," said Rhea. "When he walked in, Mrs. Biaggio didn't know who he was. He tells her he's someone who knows what happened to her husband."

"And what did Mrs. Biaggio say?"

"She cursed him," said Rhea. "Told him to get out. And he tells her that if she wants to know who stabbed her husband, then she should call him. I'm assuming he gave her a card, or something because I saw her ripping paper and putting it in the waste basket."

Suspicious, but not yet willing to jump to any conclusions, Beanie said, "That is … interesting."

"Not to the cops," quipped Rhea, rolling her eyes. "I called that detective, Janvier, and he told me that what I saw and heard was like hearsay, and since I didn't know who the guy in the leather jacket was, he had no idea who to investigate."

"What about the paper Mrs. Biaggio tore up?" asked Beanie. "You think it's still in the trashcan?"

Rhea sighed. "I don't know. Housekeeping came into the room twice since the guy in the leather jacket left."

Beanie scratched his chin. "So, not likely …"

Rhea said, "Unfortunately not …"

"Hmmm …" said Beanie, pondering what she'd told him before asking, "Are there any updates on Saul's condition? Is he still in a medically induced coma?"

Rhea nodded. "The cops showed up to talk with Mr. Biaggio's doctors a few hours ago. They wanted to know when he might wake up. They're anxious to question him, but the doctors think it might be weeks before—"

"Attentional all hospital staff, attention all hospital staff."

Beanie jumped slightly, startled by the disembodied voice as Rhea frowned.

"We have a Code Violet in ICU. Code Violet in ICU."

"Oh my God!" Rhea turned and rushed out of the waiting room.

"What's a Code Violet?" asked Beanie, following Rhea, his pulse ratcheting up as the dispatcher repeated the ominous announcement.

Glancing over her shoulder, Rhea said, "Aggressive or combative person."

Aggressive or combative person? Beanie's thoughts swirled with curiosity and anxiety as he followed Rhea. What could have caused someone to become unhinged in an ICU unit, a place where patient care was paramount? Had it been a family member disgruntled with a course of treatment? A desperate friend demanding to visit a loved one? Or, possibly a patient, confused and disoriented, unsettled and unaware of their surroundings, not sure of how they'd ended up in the hospital?

In the hallway, Rhea veered left, hurrying toward the nurse's station.

Unsure of what to do, Beanie stood paralyzed, wondering if—

Shouting and pounding footsteps, behind him, and he glanced over his shoulder. A man raced toward him, face contorted in fear, panic, and exertion, like a winger on the pitch, desperate to beat a defender and score a goal. Only the guy wasn't dressed in a jersey and shorts or wearing cleats. He looked like a businessman, dressed smart but casual —tan slacks, white dress shirt, navy blazer.

"Stop! Freeze!"

Police commands, harsh and demanding, like deafening gunshots caused panic and chaos as nurses, orderlies, and doctors scrambled to clear the way for the half dozen officers pursuing the businessman.

Jolted into action, Beanie flattened himself against a wall, trying to get out of the way. The man sprinted past him, jumping over a stretcher. The cops followed, weaving among the crash carts. The businessman grabbed an IV pole and tried to push it toward the pursuing officers, but they were able to duck and avoid the obstacles. Undeterred, the man grabbed a wheelchair and rolled it in the cops' direction, succeeding in stopping two of the police officers, who stumbled to avoid it. But the remaining cops continued after him, chasing the man around the nurses' station where he slipped, stumbling to the floor.

At once, the police converged on the man, tackling him, crashing to the floor, a mass of limbs skidding across the speckled linoleum tile. Two other officers assisted, grabbing the man's arms, yanking them behind his back, drawing shouts of protest.

"Get off me!" The man roared. "I didn't do anything!"

Wrestling with the struggling man, one of the officers cuffed him. "You're under arrest!"

"What did I do?" shouted the man, his face sweaty and florid as he continued to tussle and squirm.

The officer said, "Attempted murder!"

7

You're under arrest ... what did I do? Attempted murder!

Exhaling, Beanie tapped a pencil against his bottom lip.

Two days had passed since his visit to St. Killian General Hospital, and he was still ruminating on the businessman who'd been dragged to the floor and arrested five feet away from him. He still had no idea why the man had been apprehended. On the day in question, he hadn't been able to get much information. The police quickly yanked the man to his feet and hustled him onto the elevator. In the aftermath, the hospital staff clamored to restore order, and all non-essential workers and visitors had to leave so the doctors and nurses could make sure their most critical patients were safe and secure.

Beanie had been thinking about the man who'd been arrested since he'd written the first article about the incident. COMBATIVE HOSPITAL VISITOR ARRESTED IN ICU. He'd contacted Fields to get more details, but his friend hadn't gotten back to him. They'd agreed to meet for lunch but a liquor store robbery cancelled those plans.

Beanie's favorite food truck, located on a side street of the busy Pourciau Square, provided a bit of distraction, but the delicious goat stew ladled over coconut rice didn't stop the questions swirling in his mind.

Had the man really tried to murder someone in the ICU? And if so, why? More importantly, who?

Now, back at his small desk in his tiny cubicle at the *Palmchat Gazette*, Beanie turned his attention to the Saul Biaggio stabbing. Other than his firsthand account of the tragedy, he hadn't been able to write the follow-up articles his editor, Vivian Thomas-Bronson, demanded. As soon as possible, he needed to speak with Biaggio's wife, Tammy. So far, she'd ignored his calls. Beanie was disappointed, but not surprised. Remembering what Rhea Calais had told him, Tammy Biaggio was keeping a vigil at her husband's side, and not at all interested in talking to a reporter.

Or anyone else, he supposed, vaguely recalling something else the nurse's aide had shared with him.

Something about a man who'd pretended to be a family member in order to talk to Tammy Biaggio. Supposedly, the guy had insinuated that he had information about Saul's stabbing. But, was that true? Beanie wondered how much credit to give what amounted to unconfirmed hearsay. Rhea Calais could have been mistaken. Or maybe she hadn't understood the context of Mrs. Biaggio's conversation with the scruffy guy. Rhea had admitted to eavesdropping on a hushed conversation she could barely make out.

Beanie rubbed the back of his neck, trying to work out a knot.

But, if Rhea had heard correctly, then what? Beanie didn't want to jump to conclusions. Didn't want to assume that some mystery guy in a leather jacket knew who'd stabbed Saul Biaggio. The guy could have been trying to scam Tammy Biaggio. Promising false information in exchange for money. As sick as it was, there were perpetrators of that particular heinous fraud. People who preyed on others' grief and pain and desperate need for answers.

Turning to his computer, Beanie opened a Word document.

Time to call Tammy Biaggio again. Without the worried wife's account, the follow-up story would fall flat. Beanie couldn't sacrifice his brand with articles that amounted to a rehash of events layered between unfounded speculation. His readers counted on him to provide critical, current information. They needed to know how events affected their lives and well-being. Saul Biaggio's loan centers were crucial in various lower-end working-class neighborhoods. With Saul in a medically induced coma, people were concerned, and somewhat confused, about their outstanding debts. Who was running the company in Saul's absence? A question Beanie planned to answer as soon as he secured interviews with the staff.

Shaking his head, Beanie sighed. After he called Tammy Biaggio, who hopefully would agree to speak with him, he'd head to the breakroom for a third cup of coffee, and—

The desk phone rang.

Grabbing it, he answered, "Roland Bean."

"Hey, it's Fields," said the officer. "I'm on a break so I thought I'd give you a call about the Biaggio case."

"Great timing," said Beanie, opening a new Word doc to take additional notes. "I was about to call Tammy Biaggio to see if she'll talk to me. But, I need details for my follow-up."

"Well, as far as Tammy Biaggio is concerned," began Fields. "Janvier cleared her."

"So, she's not a suspect?"

"Mind you, Janvier has not shared all the details with me," cautioned Fields. "But, he's certain that Mrs. Biaggio couldn't have stabbed Saul because she was at home asleep when her husband was attacked."

"How is Janvier so sure of that?" questioned Beanie, fingers tapping the keyboard.

"That, I'm not sure," admitted Fields. "But if I had to guess, I'd say some sort of camera surveillance puts Tammy Biaggio at home between the hours when Saul was stabbed."

"Makes sense," said Beanie, more anxious than ever to speak with Tammy. He wanted to determine, for himself, if she truly had an alibi. Not that he was overly suspicious of Saul's wife, but with Janvier's penchant for arresting the wrong person, it was possible—probable, even—that the bumbling detective might be letting Tammy off the hook, when he needed to reel her in. After all, Saul had sputtered his wife's name before he collapsed. Had he been calling out for a cherished loved one to comfort him at a moment when he felt he might not make it? Or, had he been trying to reveal his attacker?

"Janvier also thinks Saul might have fought his attacker before he was stabbed," informed Fields. "Saul's knuckles were bruised. CSI took samples from the abrasions on his hand and scraped his nails."

"Any matches?" asked Beanie.

"They're still testing," said Fields. "Anyway, right now, Janvier is focusing on someone else." Surprised, Beanie asked, "Who?"

Fields said, "You're not going to believe this. Remember you asked me about the guy who was arrested in the ICU at St. Killian General?"

Beanie stopped typing. "The combative aggressive person who caused the Code Violet?"

"That's Janvier's main suspect."

"The man the cops arrested for attempted murder?" Beanie was shocked. "Wait a minute. He tried to kill Saul Biaggio?"

"Tried to smother him with a pillow," said Fields. "A nurse caught him. He's still in jail."

"Who is he?" asked Beanie. "Why did he try to kill Saul?"

"Not sure why he tried to kill Biaggio," said Fields. "But his name is Quincy Irving and he's got an interesting connection to Saul."

"What do you mean?"

"Quincy Irving was the CFO of Saul's company, Biaggio Loans Inc."

8

"I didn't stab Saul," insisted Quincy Irving, his dark eyes wide and intense behind the wire-rimmed glasses sitting on the bridge of his large, beak-like nose. Dressed in a rumpled, faded orange jumpsuit, Irving looked nothing like the smart businessman who'd barreled down the ICU hallway at St. Killian General. Haggard and harried, he appeared sallow, like he was recovering from a massive hangover.

Beanie stared at the former Chief Financial Officer of Biaggio Loans, Inc., who'd agreed to a jailhouse interview in order to, in his words, set the record straight and make sure his side of the narrative was reported correctly. Yesterday, after his conversation with Fields, Beanie had headed to Vivian's office to update her with the details he'd learned. Not surprisingly, Vivian wanted him to talk to Irving while he was still behind bars and she used her connections to make it happen.

Today, after his second cup of coffee and a quick conference with his boss, Beanie headed to the jail facilities at the St. Killian Police Department. After going through the prerequisite security procedures, he went to the visiting room and sat in one of the booths. Moments later, Irving sat down on the opposite side of the Plexiglass and picked up the phone. When Beanie brought the phone to his ear, before he could introduce himself, Irving started protesting his arrest and professing his innocence.

Beanie said, "But you did try to smother Saul with a pillow."

Quincy Irving shook his head. "I didn't do that, either."

Beanie suppressed a sigh. He hadn't expected Irving to confess, considering the man was giving a jailhouse interview that was being surveilled and recorded. Still, the constant denials wouldn't make good copy. He had to find a way to coax or even trick, the man into giving him something interesting. If not an exclusive scoop, then at least a juicy nugget to keep his readers intrigued.

"What exactly did you do?" asked Beanie.

Irving sighed, scratching his thick, wiry salt-and-pepper beard. "I went to the hospital to visit Saul. I'd read your story about Saul being stabbed. I wanted to make sure he was okay. So, I went to the ICU."

"Normally, only family members can visit patients in the ICU."

"That's why I didn't tell anyone I wanted to see him," said Irving. "I slipped into his room when no one was looking. I walked over to him and I whispered his name. Told him it was me and told him I wanted to see how he was doing. And that's when he opened his eyes and he tried to speak."

Skeptical, Beanie said, "Saul is in a medically induced coma. There's no way he could have opened his eyes and spoken to you."

Shrugging, Irving looked away for a moment, then back to Beanie. "At least I thought he did. I'm sure he did."

Not bothering to hide his doubt, Beanie said, "And what did Saul say?"

"He was mumbling. Moaning," said Irving, clutching the phone receiver. "I thought he might have been in distress. It seemed to me as though the angle of his body on the hospital bed was odd and I wondered if maybe his neck might be stiff, and I didn't want him to be in pain, so I …"

"You … what?" Prompted Beanie, thinking he might be amused by Irving's blatant lies if the story wasn't so ridiculous and pathetic.

Clearing his throat, and looking away, Irving shrugged. "So I pulled the pillow from under Saul's head, and that's when the nurse came in and misunderstood what was happening."

"The nurse misunderstood?"

Irving nodded. "She mistakenly believed I was trying to hurt Saul, but nothing could be further from the truth."

"So what's the truth?" asked Beanie, quite certain that whatever Irving told him would be the furthest thing from the truth, but as a journalist, he had to keep his opinions to himself, as always, in an attempt to remain objective.

"The truth is that I considered Saul a very good friend," insisted Irving. "He's been a mentor to me. Someone who has always supported my career, great to work with, and sure, recently, we've had some differences, but …"

Beanie perked up as Irving piped down. "What kind of differences have you had with Saul?"

Looking away again, Irving said, "Look, I need to get back to my cell, but just make sure you report the truth. I didn't stab Saul. I would never hurt him."

"Can you tell me more about the differences you and—"

Expelling a low grunt, Quincy Irving slammed the receiver down, jumped up, and hurried away.

9

"Would you like anything to drink? Water? Coffee?" The receptionist gave him a polite smile.

"No, thank you," declined Beanie. "I'm fine."

But that wasn't exactly true.

Standing in the offices of Biaggio Loans, Inc., what he felt was the very opposite of fine. Spooked? Worried? Apprehensive? Yes. All three. He told himself to get over it. Get past it. Get through it. He was being unnecessarily dramatic. He was here to do a job. Get information, which he needed since Vivian wanted a follow-up to the Quincy Irving arrest story, which had done well.

In the two days since the article had been published, the story had proved pretty popular on the paper's website and social media accounts. The likes, shares, and comments had led to more subscribers to the *Palmchat Gazette*'s paid online version.

Unfortunately, not much progress had been made in the investigation. The crime scene techs were still analyzing the DNA found in Saul Biaggio's cuts and abrasions, reviewing hotel surveillance, and scouring CCTV video of the streets surrounding the Oyster Farms area, hoping to find some sign of Saul Biaggio on camera, trying to determine how the man had ended up in Beanie's backyard.

Detective Janvier was convinced that Quincy Irving had not only attempted to murder Saul in the ICU at St, Killian General but had stabbed the man in the early morning of the new year. Despite having no evidence to prove his suspicions, according to Fields, Janvier was convinced that Irving had gone to the ICU to finish Saul off after learning the man hadn't succumbed to the stab wounds.

Following Quincy Irving's arrest, Beanie decided to interview Saul Biaggio's staff for more insight into Irving. The suspect's coworkers might have information that could reveal motives and even clues that led to the truth. If nothing else, Beanie hoped to get the staff's thoughts on Irving's arrest. Did they believe Quincy Irving had tried to kill Saul? And if so, why?

The executive team at Biaggio Loans, Inc. wasn't exactly keen to speak with Beanie, and it had taken a few days to get them to agree to an interview. Today, Beanie was scheduled to talk with Biaggio's Chief Operating Officer and the company's Controller.

However, if Beanie had known Biaggio's company was located in suite 308 of the Pourciau building, he might have requested to meet elsewhere.

Anywhere except the former offices of S.O.R.E., Inc.

"Okay, you can take a seat and I'll let Ms. Javon know you're here," said the receptionist.

As he took a seat in the waiting room, he shuddered. But it wasn't the A/C or the palmetto-shaped ceiling fans whirling above him that caused the chill. S.O.R.E., Inc., founded and owned by a twisted con artist named Venus L'Amour, claimed to be a center devoted to helping men recover from mental issues. The truth was much darker, more sinister. And deadly.

Beanie scratched his chin.

S.O.R.E., Inc. was no longer in business, and L'Amour was behind bars. Beanie suspected the office had been redecorated. Still, he couldn't help thinking that heinous spirits lingered. He wasn't superstitious but the place gave him bad vibes, despite its sunny, beachy décor.

Several minutes later, the receptionist announced that she would escort him to the conference room, where the executive team would answer his questions. After a quick walk down a long hall, Beanie entered a large rectangular space with glass walls that offered sweeping views of Pourciau Square.

The executive team stood at the far opposite end of the conference table. The COO, a slender, pale young woman with dull red hair slicked back and wrapped in a bun at the nape of her neck, was dressed in a pencil skirt, short-sleeved blouse, and ballet flats. She had light brown doe-like eyes and a wide, thin-lipped smile that was more polite than genuine. On her right was a muscular man of medium height, wearing a velvet tracksuit and a thick gold chain around his neck. Not exactly business attire, thought Beanie.

Sensing their reluctance, which they barely hid behind blank stares, Beanie took a quick deep breath and approached with a broad smile and his extended hand. In short order, introductions were made.

The Controller thrust his hand toward Beanie.

"Ivan Rublev," he said, with a slight Eastern European accent.

Before grabbing Rublev's hand, Beanie as he noticed the three flashy, gaudy diamond rings, one yellow, one pink, and one pale green, adorning his fingers, pushed past knuckles which appeared bruised, with several micro-cuts.

"And I'm Saul's COO, Lisette Javon," said the redhead, offering him a limp handshake.

Without thinking, Beanie glanced at her hand. No ostentatious diamonds, but she did have a birthmark resembling a raspberry-colored splotch stretched across the back of her pale hand.

"Thank you for agreeing to speak with me," said Beanie, taking a seat next to Lisette Javon, directly across from Ivan Rublev.

"No problem," said Lisette. "We're happy to—"

"Before we start," said Ivan Rublev, frowning. "You have any idea how long this is going to take? Because I have reports to finish."

Beanie cleared his throat. "Well—"

"What happened to Saul was awful," said Rublev, leaning back in his leather seat. "But Lisette and I have a lot of work to do."

Lisette added, "And we would appreciate it if, in your story, you make it clear that the company is fine. We are working diligently and maintaining productivity."

"We can't have people losing confidence in the business," said Rublev.

"No, of course not," said Beanie. "I won't take up too much of your time, I promise. I'd just like to know your thoughts about—"

"I am afraid that we may waste your time," said Rublev. "We don't have much to add to the story. Neither Lisette nor I know anything about what happened to Saul."

"Have you spoken to the police?" asked Beanie, glancing at Lisette, who seemed content letting Rublev speak for her. Beanie wondered if, in advance of his arrival, they'd decided Rublev would assert any official statements. Maybe. But that didn't mean Lisette agreed with the official statement. What might she say if Rublev wasn't around?

"We have both given statements," confirmed Rublev. "Did you read them? Can't you just consult the statements we gave the cops?"

"I'd prefer to hear what each of you have to say," said Beanie, sensing that Ivan Rublev was becoming increasingly irritated. Beanie shared the man's frustration. He had a feeling the Controller was right. This would be a waste of time.

"But, that's just it," said Rublev. "We don't have anything to say. That's what we told the cops. We don't know anything."

"Did you all attend the New Year's Eve party?" asked Beanie.

"We both did, yes," confirmed Rublev. "It was a great party. We all had a good time."

"And I'm assuming Quincy Irving attended, as well," said Beanie.

Lisette said, "No, he didn't."

"Why not?"

"Saul had to let him go," said Lisette. "So, once his employment was terminated, his invitation was rescinded."

"He was very angry about that," said Rublev.

Shifting in his seat, Beanie asked, "Why was Mr. Irving fired?"

"Because he is a cold-blooded thief," announced Rublev, his icy stare intense.

Lisette cleared her throat. "I wouldn't say that. And, Mr. Bean, I hope you won't print that as there is no proof that—"

"You know it is true," insisted Rublev, leaving over the table. "Saul would not have fired Quincy if his suspicions were not valid."

"Saul thought Quincy Irving was stealing from him?" asked Beanie, trying to understand the allegations against Irving.

Sighing, Lisette said, "Saul believed that Quincy Irving was using the company to launder money."

"I discovered several financial discrepancies in Quincy's reporting," said Rublev, leaning back in his chair, his expression smug. "There was only one conclusion as Quincy is not a stupid man. He is very proficient at his job, very smart. I shared my suspicions with Saul, and he agreed with me. However, there is still more proof to uncover. There is a money trail to follow. There are other bad actors to expose."

"Other bad actors?"

Lisette said, "Saul suspected Quincy was laundering money for some criminal organization. Maybe the PC-5."

Processing the interesting allegations, Beanie stroked his jaw, making a mental note to speak to Lime Shoes.

Rublev said, "If you want a comment for your story, you can report that I believe the police have arrested the right person. Quincy tried to kill Saul because Saul fired him and was planning to inform the police of his crimes. Quincy would have lost everything and gone to jail. His life would have been ruined. He attacked Saul to make sure he would not have to pay for his crimes."

It was a compelling motive, Beanie thought, if it was true. But Lisette Javon had pointed out that while Saul was skeptical of Quincy Irving, he'd lacked proof of Irving's money laundering scheme.

Beanie said, "But, as far as I know, there's no evidence—other than an ICU nurse's statement that she believed Quincy Irving was trying to smother Saul with a pillow—that Irving attacked Saul. No proof that Irving stabbed Saul."

Leaning forward again, Rublev said, "This is all the proof you, and the police, need: the day before New Year's Eve, when Saul fired Quincy, they had a big blow-up in Saul's office."

Beanie glanced at Lisette, who nodded, confirming Rublev's assertion.

"Before Saul told Quincy to leave and never return," said Rublev, "Quincy told Saul that he would pay for firing him. And I believe Quincy made good on that threat when he stabbed Saul in the gut."

10

A lone person occupied the quiet ICU waiting room.

This morning, Beanie was back at St. Killian General Hospital, trying again to talk to Tammy Biaggio, after being ignored for the past few days. Technically, this was waylaying the witness, but he needed her comment to add to his next follow-up article. His story about Quincy Irving, *BIAGGIO EMPLOYEE ACCUSED OF ATTEMPTED MURDER* had done well, with lots of engagement, comments, shares, and likes. Considering Irving's arrest, Beanie was curious about Tammy's thoughts concerning her husband's chief financial officer trying to kill him. He also wanted to ask her about the difficulties with Saul that Irving alluded to before he abruptly ended the jailhouse interview. Turned out, those difficulties had to do with Saul suspecting Irving of laundering money and then firing him. Did Tammy know anything about that?

Beanie stared at the dark-haired woman wearing sunglasses, dressed in what Beanie suspected was a designer pantsuit, perched on the edge of a couch near the far-left corner. With her opulent, moneyed demeanor, Beanie figured she was Tammy Biaggio. In addition to the fancy duds, she sported a diamond on her finger that was as big as a beach pebble, and a matching tennis bracelet which she pulled at, circling it around and around her wrist. The repetitive action suggested it was something done to distract or soothe herself.

With cautious steps, Beanie approached her. "Mrs. Biaggio?"

Her body jerked slightly, and then she tilted her head toward him. "Who are you?"

"My name is Roland Bean," said Beanie, taking the seat perpendicular to the couch. "I'm with the *Palmchat Gazette*. I'd like to ask you a few questions if you don't mind."

She looked away. "Questions about what?"

"About what happened to your husband," said Beanie.

Tammy Biaggio shook her head, then angled her body away from him, and continued to pick at her dazzling diamond bracelet.

The cold shoulder. Beanie had received it from witnesses and persons of interest and potential sources before. Normally, he could find a way to cajole a person into talking to him. But he had a feeling Tammy Biaggio would be a stubborn goat, as his grandfather would say. In the Palmchat Islands, there was a proverb that went something like, that goat ain't going to eat grass.

Beanie needed to break through Mrs. Biaggio's resistance and reluctance. Vivian wanted a story featuring Tammy Biaggio on her desk before the end of the day. Despite his own resistance and reluctance, Beanie would have to bring out the big guns.

Clearing his throat, Beanie said, "Mrs. Biaggio, I just want to tell you that I hope your husband will pull through. I'm not sure if the police told you, but your husband collapsed in my backyard."

Her head whipped toward him, thick dark hair swishing around her shoulders. "What?"

Nodding, Beanie said, "Mr. Biaggio somehow climbed over the fence into my backyard and—"

"So, he really was found in Oyster Farms?" Shaking her head, Tammy Biaggio said, "I told the police that was impossible. My husband has never been to that neighborhood in his life. I'm not sure he knows anything about Oyster Farms. He's not from the Palmchat Islands."

"And you are?" asked Beanie, though he recognized her accent.

"I grew up in Little Turkey." She nodded. "Oyster Farms. I wonder how he got there."

"So you don't know?"

"The only thing I know is I went to bed with my husband and I woke up to the police at my door telling me Saul had been stabbed, then taken to the hospital, went through emergency surgery, and was placed in a medically induced coma."

Several questions swirled in Beanie's mind, but he started with, "What time did you and Mr. Biaggio turn in for the night?"

Pulling the bracelet around her wrist, Tammy Biaggio said, "I'll tell you what I told the police. Saul and I host a New Year's Eve party every year. After the party ended, Saul and I left the Queen Palm around two-fifteen in the morning. We'd rented the main ballroom until two a.m. So, the valets bring Saul's Rolls around. We get in and drive off. I curled up in my seat and closed my eyes. We'd had a great party, but I was tired so Saul told me to rest and he'd wake me up when we got home. But we never made it home."

"You didn't make it home?"

"No, no, that's not what I meant to say." Pressing the bridge of her nose, Tammy said, "Please be patient with me. I've hardly slept, I'm terrified for Saul, my mind is all over the place, and—"

"No, it's fine," assured Beanie. "Please, just take your time."

After a deep, shuddering exhale, Tammy continued. "I was dozing when I heard Saul cursing, saying something like, an idiot was riding his tail. I opened my eyes and turned to look out the back window. I saw a car following too close behind us. The headlights nearly blinded me. Saul started driving faster, but the car was keeping up. I was terrified, thinking we were going to be run off the road and carjacked. Saul said he was going to lose the guy, so he turned off the coast road and headed downtown."

Beanie pictured the downtown St. Killian layout, a dense grid of brick paved roads, short, narrow streets, and tight turns where an experienced driver might be able to shake a tail.

"Saul kept driving faster, trying to lose the car behind us," continued Tammy. "But then, all of a sudden, he jerked the Rolls over to the curb and slammed on his brakes. I was so scared. Why did he stop? Saul said, it's Ken."

"Ken?"

"Kenneth Moreaux." Tammy nodded. "Saul's former business partner."

Beanie was shocked. "Kenneth Moreaux was following you?"

"Kenneth Moreaux was trying to run us off the road," snapped Tammy. "Saul must have recognized Ken's car. I told him to call the police but he didn't want to do that."

"What did Saul want to do?"

Jumping up, Tammy paced the length of the couch. "He wanted to get out and talk to Ken. I didn't want Saul to do that. We went back and forth and then the next thing I know, Ken is beating his fists against Saul's window. He looks crazy. Like a madman. He's yelling at Saul to get out of the car."

"And Saul got out?" asked Beanie, wishing he could record the conversation, or at least use his phone to take notes, but he didn't want Mrs. Biaggio to remember that she didn't want to make a statement and stop talking to him.

"I begged him not to," said Tammy. "But Saul said he wasn't afraid of him. He said he wanted to talk Ken down."

"Talk him down?"

"Saul thought Ken was having an episode," said Tammy. "Ken hasn't been right in the head since his accident. He slammed into that tree and wasn't the same. He became violent. Acted like a crazy man."

Beanie scratched his jaw, recalling what his neighbor, Mendez, had told him about Kenneth Moreaux's car accident.

"After Saul got out, I got out, too," said Tammy. "Ken was shouting and cursing. I thought he might hurt Saul. So, then I—"

"Mrs. Biaggio …"

At the interruption, Beanie glanced over his shoulder. An ICU nurse stood at the waiting room entrance. "The doctor would like to talk to you now."

"I'm afraid I have to go," said Tammy, eyes haunted, face pale.

"I understand, but before you do," said Beanie. "What do you think about Quincy Irving being arrested for attacking Saul?"

Her mouth set in a grim, tight line, Tammy said, "I think the police arrested the wrong man. Quincy didn't stab Saul. Why would he?"

"Saul fired him the day before New Year's Eve," said Beanie. "Did you know that? Saul suspected Quincy Irving of laundering money."

"Saul had no proof of that," said Tammy. "Those were Ivan Rublev's suspicions. But, even if it was true, and I don't think Quincy laundered money, he would not have attacked Saul. As I told the police, they need to focus on Ken, but that detective won't listen to me."

Beanie stared at Tammy Biaggio. "You think Kenneth Moreaux stabbed Saul?"

"I'm sure of it," insisted Tammy Biaggio. "Ken is crazy and he tried to kill my husband."

11

Ken is crazy and he tried to kill my husband …

Shaking his head, Beanie leaned back in the chair at his tiny desk in his small cubicle at the *Palmchat Gazette* offices. A few days ago, when he'd met with the executive team at Biaggio Loan, Inc., and they'd shared their suspicions of Quincy Irving, Beanie had been willing to concede that if Irving had been laundering money, and if Saul was close to uncovering evidence to prove the malfeasance, then Irving had a compelling motive to go after Saul.

Beanie had theorized that point in his follow-up article, BIAGGIO STAFF POINTS FINGER AT EX-CFO.

But this afternoon, following his interview with Tammy Biaggio at the hospital, Beanie had to consider Saul's ex-business partner, Kenneth Moreaux, as a viable suspect. Beanie floated that speculation in the article he'd drafted moments ago, tentatively headlined: LOAN KING'S WIFE SUSPECTS FORMER PARTNER.

After emailing the draft to Vivian, he'd enticed his coworkers Stevie and Caleb for a late afternoon respite in the breakroom, where he lured them into a speculation session. The two men, polar opposites in every way imaginable, had always provided a good sounding board for Beanie's deductions and theories.

Stevie, the scion of the billionaire island family responsible for brewing Felipe Beer and distilling the most expensive, exclusive top-shelf rum in the world, was a slacker with a surfer's attitude but a surprisingly sharp mind. Caleb, the seniormost reporter, who never let anyone forget it, was grumpy and ill-tempered, but possessed a wealth of wisdom and knowledge that was indispensable—when he was in the mood to share that wisdom and knowledge.

Shrugging and scowling, Caleb said, "It's looking to me like Quincy Irving did it. He was laundering money. Saul fired him. He decided to get back at Saul."

"But there's no proof that Irving laundered money," countered Beanie. "There seems to be only suspicion and speculation."

"If Saul fired Irving," said Stevie. "Then I think there was more than just suspicion."

Conceding that Stevie had a point, Beanie said, "Fair. Irving has a motive for wanting Saul dead. And it's possible that he tried to kill Saul —at the hospital. I definitely don't believe Irving's story about trying to readjust Saul's pillow to make him more comfortable."

"Neither do I," said Stevie.

"But I also don't think Irving stabbed Saul," said Beanie.

"You believe Tammy Biaggio?" asked Caleb. "You think Kenneth Moreaux stabbed Saul?"

"It's definitely more plausible, and more probable," said Beanie. "Tammy claims that Moreaux followed them through the streets of downtown St. Killian until Saul recognized it was Moreaux behind him."

"But Tammy didn't tell you that Moreaux stabbed Saul," pointed out Stevie.

"She didn't get a chance to," said Beanie. "Our conversation was interrupted by a nurse who told Tammy the doctor wanted to speak with her."

Caleb shook his head. "I don't think she was going to tell you that Moreaux stabbed Saul."

"Why not?" asked Beanie.

"Because if he had, Tammy Biaggio would have told the cops that," said Caleb. "And Janvier would have arrested Moreaux."

"You're right," said Beanie, taking another sip of coffee.

Stevie said, "I don't think Tammy knows who stabbed Saul. Remember, you said she told you that they made it home."

"But before that, they got run off the road by Kenneth Moreaux, who got out of his car, seemingly to confront Saul," said Beanie.

"Wonder why he did that?" asked Stevie.

"Word is, Moreaux has beef with Saul because Saul kicked him out of the company they built together," said Caleb.

Nodding Beanie said, "My neighbor reminded me about Moreaux's car accident. Apparently, he suffered a brain injury that caused mood swings. And Tammy said Saul thought Ken was having an episode."

Caleb said, "I don't know too much about the mood swings. But I do know that Moreaux was mad as a wet nanny goat when Saul forced him out of the company."

"Mad enough to try to kill Saul?" asked Stevie.

Caleb shrugged and stood. "I can't say that for sure. But Moreaux was mad enough to sue Saul."

Fifteen minutes later, back at his desk, Beanie thought more about Kenneth Moreaux. Had Saul's former partner tried to kill him? After talking to his colleagues, Beanie decided that he wasn't ready to believe Moreaux was guilty. And he was curious about the lawsuit Moreaux had brought against Saul.

Turning to his computer, Beanie executed a public record search of Kenneth Moreaux, including a civil case search. Most of the interesting facts came from the legal documents on file with the local courthouse.

The petitioner, Moreaux, had accused the defendant, Biaggio, of perpetrating fraud against him by engaging in criminal business practices. There were allegations of stealing company funds, embezzlement, and falsifying financial records and reports to defraud investors and clients. From his testimony against Biaggio, Moreaux appeared to be a bitter, disgruntled ex-partner determined to bring Biaggio to his knees, even if he had to lie to do it.

As Beanie printed the documents he'd researched, his thoughts drifted to an image of Saul staggering in his backyard, bleeding from a stab wound. Had Moreaux stabbed Saul? If so, when? If Tammy Biaggio was to be believed, she and Saul eventually returned home following the altercation with Moreaux. Beanie doubted that Moreaux had stabbed Saul after forcing the man to pull over to the side of the road.

If that had happened, Tammy would have called an ambulance. Or driven her husband to the emergency room. So, had Saul been stabbed after he'd arrived home? If so, then how did Saul end up in Oyster Farms?

Beanie rubbed his jaw. Too many questions. Not enough information to speculate or form any conclusions at this point.

However, he believed Moreaux probably had a motive to want Saul dead. Moreaux probably felt betrayed by Saul. But did Moreaux have means? So far, the police had not recovered the knife used to stab Saul. And what about opportunity? If Tammy and Saul made it home after the incident with Moreaux, then it meant Saul was stabbed … when? Beanie didn't know the timeline. He'd have to ask Fields. But if it turned out that Moreaux had an alibi for the time when the police believed Saul was stabbed … then what?

Questions about Moreaux swirled in Beanie's mind.

And the only way to get answers was to talk to the man …

12

As he made another pass across the lawn with the mower, Beanie was thankful for a breezy, overcast Saturday morning. The buzzing hum of the lawnmower blended with the mechanical whirring, clacking, and whining of various other yard tools. Like many of his neighbors, weekends were for yard work, gardening, and minor household renovations.

He glanced up at the low cloud deck, wondering if it might rain later in the afternoon. Hopefully, he'd be finished with the grass, hedges, and bushes before any tropical showers. With Noelle and the boys still lounging around following breakfast, he could get the yard maintenance accomplished.

Which brought to mind another task he had yet to accomplish.

An interview with Kenneth Moreaux.

A few days had passed since his conversation with Tammy Biaggio. Beanie was eager to get a comment from Saul's ex-partner about Tammy's allegations, but so far, Moreaux was not returning his calls or responding to his emails.

Beanie had contacted Fields to find out what Janvier thought about Tammy Biaggio's story and was not surprised to learn that the detective was still convinced that Quincy Irving was the main suspect. So far,

Janvier hadn't found any CCTV footage to corroborate Tammy's claim that Kenneth Moreaux had forced the Rolls off the road. However, CCTV was often unreliable. Often, the cameras didn't work, or were disabled, for some reason.

Walking behind the self-propelled mower, Beanie's thoughts drifted to Quincy Irving.

Beanie agreed that Quincy Irving had probably tried to finish Saul off while the man was lying comatose in the ICU. Irving's abrupt termination gave the man a motive. But if the man had also stabbed Saul in the early hours of the new year, then when had he done it? And how? And why would Irving have stabbed Saul in Oyster Farms?

Thinking about Quincy Irving made Beanie remember that he wanted to talk to the man about the money laundering accusations. And he should probably reach out to the Biaggio Loans, Inc. staff again. Find out their opinions about Kenneth Moreaux. Did they think the man could have attacked Saul?

Beanie pivoted the mower to make another pass in the opposite direction.

Mr. Mendez, his George Hamilton lookalike neighbor, walked up the driveway, waving and calling his name.

Groaning, Beanie finished the strip of grass in the path of the mower, then cut the machine off. He wasn't in the mood to chit-chat with Mendez. Completing the yard work before it rained, or conversely, before the cluster of gray clouds floated away to reveal a scorching hot sun, was his most pressing objective. Mendez likely wanted to impart inconsequential gossip, which Beanie knew he would have no interest in. Nevertheless, in the interest of being neighborly, he would take a quick break.

"Beanie, my friend!" called out Mendez. "How are you?"

"Doing good," said Beanie, wiping sweat from his brow with the back of his hand. "I'll be doing a lot better when the yard is done."

"I hear you," said Mendez, nodding. "You've got it looking good, so far. I envy you. I would do my yard myself but I have bad knees. So, I hire some guys. Costs a fortune, but it's either that or I'll be stiff the rest of the week."

Beanie chuckled. "I understand. While I can manage it, I'll do the lawn and save a bit of money."

"Hey, listen, I know you need to get back to your work," said Mendez, "but I read what Biaggio's wife said in that article you wrote, and I got to thinking maybe she's right about Moreaux. Considering Saul was in the back of Moreaux's place the night he was stabbed."

"Saul was in the back of Moreaux's place?"

Mendez nodded. "Did you know that the house directly behind yours belongs to Kenneth Moreaux? It's on Porpoise Circle."

Porpoise Circle was the cul-de-sac behind Dolphin Lane, the street where Beanie and Mendez lived.

"I had no idea," said Beanie, his interest piqued.

"So, you know what that means," said Mendez, voice lowered. "When Saul jumped the fence into your backyard, he had been in the backyard of one of Moreaux's rental houses."

Beanie understood where his neighbor was going with the information.

"You have to wonder," continued Mendez. "What was Saul doing in the backyard of Moreaux's house? How did he get there? Was that where he was stabbed?"

Exhaling, Beanie wiped sweat from his brow. Mendez's revelation shed new light on things. Janvier wasn't giving much credit to Tammy's version of events, but Beanie wondered if, somehow, Saul and Moreaux met up again, after Saul arrived home. Maybe Moreaux asked Saul to meet him at his rental property. Tammy had mentioned Saul believed that Moreaux needed to be calmed down from an "episode" he was having. Obviously, despite kicking Moreaux out of the company, Saul probably still considered Moreaux a friend. Still cared about Moreaux's well-being.

Could Moreaux have tricked Saul into a meeting at the rental house? Maybe he'd told Saul he wanted help dealing with a mental issue? Something related to the brain injury he'd sustained from the accident. Saul might have agreed, fearing Moreaux might do something devastating, like hurt himself. But, unbeknownst to Saul, Moreaux might have been lying in wait, ready to ambush the partner he'd felt betrayed him.

"Is the house occupied?" asked Beanie.

Mendez shook his head. "It's empty. The family that was staying there moved out about three months ago."

Beanie sighed again. His theory about Moreaux tricking Saul to attack him seemed more and more plausible.

"So, you know I've got my surveillance system," said Mendez. "Well, I've got a friend on Porpoise Circle who has a setup similar to mind. So, I called him to ask him to review his footage from New Year's Eve."

"Did he see anything?" asked Beanie.

"He hasn't been able to review it because he's in the UK visiting his grandkids," said Mendez. "His system is closed-circuit, like mine, so it can't be hacked. Which is good. Only, in this case, it's not, because what if Saul's attacker is on that footage?"

"Did your friend call the police?" asked Beanie. "Maybe he can give them access to his home and permission to take a look at the surveillance."

"That's a good idea," said Mendez. "I'll give him a call and advise him to do that. In the meantime …"

"What?" asked Beanie, searching his neighbor's face.

His expression forlorn, Mendez said, "I got to ask you. Do you think Moreaux tried to kill Biaggio? I sure hope not. And if he did, had to be because his mind is not right, you know? Moreaux is a good guy. Hate to see him locked up if he didn't have possession of his faculties."

Beanie said, "I'm not sure. It's too soon to tell. Too soon to speculate. We need more information."

An hour or so later, after he'd finished the yard, Beanie stood in his backyard, drinking a bottle of water and staring at the fence. The fence Saul had managed to jump over in his desperate search for help. The fence separating Beanie's yard from Moreaux's yard.

He'd told Mendez more information was needed before they could conclude that Kenneth Moreaux was guilty. He'd meant they needed evidence that Moreaux had attacked Mendez. Could there be evidence on the other side of the fence that proved Kenneth Moreaux stabbed Saul?

Beanie took another sip of water. The only way to find out was to go on the other side of the fence.

Minutes later, wearing work gloves, Beanie grabbed the top of the six-foot high fence and paused. Was he actually about to climb the fence? Could he actually climb the fence? As a teenager, he'd climbed plenty of fences. But that was fifteen years ago. And, technically, climbing over his fence into Moreaux's backyard was trespassing.

But, he wanted to look for evidence.

Not that he knew what he was looking for, or if he would find anything.

With a sigh, Beanie jumped to hoist himself onto the planks, using his momentum to walk up the fence until he was able to swing one leg over, straddle the fence, and then, still keeping a firm grip on the top, lower his other leg over and jump down.

Landing on the grass, which seemed to have been recently cut, Beanie faced the back of the rental house. Like his own home, Moreaux's place was modern and modest, most likely the same open concept two bedroom, two bath plan.

Surveying the yard, Beanie stared at the expanse of grass surrounding a small, square patio. The lack of outdoor furniture made sense. Most tenants would probably want to bring their own decorations. With the faint sounds of passing cars, laughing kids, and island music, he headed toward the patio, focusing on the glass doors.

The wide panes reflected the afternoon sunlight. Stepping onto the paver stones, he inspected the glass as he walked toward it. Nothing seemed broken. He checked the handle. The patio door was locked. But that didn't mean that Moreaux hadn't opened it and then closed and locked it behind him after stabbing Saul and leaving him to collapse and bleed out in the grass.

Was that how it happened?

Maybe Moreaux and Saul argued in the backyard? Moreaux probably hadn't wanted to stab Saul in the house. Not if he wanted to rent the house again. Didn't need his new tenants noticing blood on the carpet. Beanie pressed his gloved hands against the glass, then peered closer to look inside the house.

From the patio, the doors opened into the dining room and kitchen, both of which were empty. If there had been any furniture in the house, there might have been signs of a struggle. A broken vase. An overturned flowerpot, dirt spilling across the floor. Chairs tipped onto their sides.

But, maybe not. If Moreaux had attacked Saul in a furnished house, the man would probably have cleaned up the place. Tried to get rid of any evidence.

Sighing, Beanie faced the yard.

But why would Moreaux lure Saul to his rental house to stab him? It was too risky. Surely, the police had made the same connections Mendez had. Saul Biaggio had been in the backyard of a rental house that belonged to Kenneth Moreaux. What did the police think about that? What did Janvier think? Beanie would have to ask Fields.

In any event, it didn't make sense for Moreaux to stab Saul at his rental property. Moreaux had to know the police would have questions for him. The cops would investigate his house.

The problem was, Moreaux had been doing lots of things that didn't make sense, since his accident.

Beanie paced the patio, staring at the pavers, looking for anything that might seem suspicious. He wondered if Moreaux hadn't meant to stab Saul. Perhaps the attack had been a burst of wild rage. After suffering his injury, apparently, Moreaux had behaved in a chaotic, deranged manner. Both Tammy and Mendez had said Moreaux wasn't in his right mind.

Pinching the bridge of his nose, Beanie stepped off the patio.

First thing Monday morning, he would call Fields to ask if the police had searched the rental property and if so, then—

A glint in the grass caught his eye.

Blinking, Beanie stared at the shorn blades, focusing, trying to determine where he'd seen the glint of light. And wondering if he'd actually seen it. And if he had, what could it have been? He took a few cautious steps, eyes on the ground, trying to—

Another quick flash, to his left.

Taking a knee in the grass, Beanie removed the glove from his right hand. Inching his fingers slowly toward the blades, he flattened them, exposing what he'd seen sparking in the afternoon sun.

Beanie picked up the object.

Confused, he stared at the white gold cable link chain, on the end of which was what had caught the sunlight.

A diamond solitaire pendant.

13

Driving away from the *Palmchat Gazette* on a windy afternoon, Beanie maneuvered through the streets of downtown St. Killian, every now and then checking for CCTV cameras, wondering about the route Saul Biaggio had driven as he tried to shake Kenneth Moreaux's tail.

Beanie took the traffic circle, his thoughts drifting to his conversation with Officer Damon Fields earlier that morning. They'd met for a quick coffee at Pourciau Square. Beanie had been anxious to share the clue he'd found in Kenneth Moreaux's backyard.

Fields had been reluctant to take possession of the diamond necklace; which Beanie had placed in a plastic sandwich bag for safekeeping until he could talk with the officer.

"And what makes you think this necklace has anything to do with what happened to Saul Biaggio?"

Undeterred by Fields' hesitation, Beanie ignored his coffee, sitting on the small bistro table they'd found in the park. "It's like I told you—"

"Yeah, yeah, I know your theory," said Fields, frowning. "You think Moreaux could have lured Saul to the rental house and stabbed him in the backyard? It's plausible. Good luck getting Janvier to get on board with it, but I can imagine it might have gone down like that. Still a long way from proving it and there are still a lot of holes. But, again, I ask, what does this necklace have to do with anything?"

Beanie hadn't known what to tell Fields.

What *did* the necklace have to do with Saul Biaggio's stabbing? Maybe everything. But most likely, nothing at all. And as Fields had pointed out, the necklace could have been accidentally lost in the grass by a former tenant. But Fields was more concerned with how Beanie had come into possession of the necklace.

"You trespassed on private property," said Fields, a hint of censure in his tone. "Even if the necklace could lead to finding out who stabbed Biaggio, it probably can't be used in court because it's tainted. Evidence obtained illegally is not admissible."

Beanie understood. For all anyone knew, Beanie could have been lying about finding the necklace in the backyard, which was probably what Janvier would think. Nevertheless, Fields agreed to mention the necklace to the detective. Beanie doubted that anything would come from the clue he'd found. If it really was a clue.

His current endeavor would hopefully yield better results.

Once again, he was going to interview Quincy Irving, the former CFO of Biaggio Loans, Inc., but this morning, he wasn't heading to the jail at the St. Killian Police Department. Irving had been released on bond a few days ago and was under house arrest at his home in Adagio Bay.

Irving had agreed to the interview after Beanie informed him about the money laundering claims.

"Thank you for talking to me, Mr. Irving," said Beanie, stepping over the threshold into Irving's condo in the five-story luxury building overlooking the marina.

"I only agreed because I don't want you printing lies about me," said Irving, slamming the front door before stomping into the living area.

Exhaling, Beanie tempered his frustration, preparing himself for a hostile witness. "Well, it's not my intention to print any lies so I'm happy to get your side of the story."

"What is this nonsense about me laundering money?" demanded

Irving, walking to a wet bar where he opened a bottle of rum and poured it into a tumbler.

Beanie said, "I spoke with your former coworker, Ivan Rublev—"

"You can't believe a word that mobster tells you," growled Irving.

"Mobster?" asked Beanie, taking a seat on a chair adjacent to the couch.

"Rublev is Russian mafia," said Irving. "You want a drink?"

"No, I'm on the clock," said Beanie, somewhat stunned by Irving's claims about Ivan Rublev.

"Suit yourself," said Irving, walking to the couch, dropping down onto the middle cushion.

"What makes you think Ivan Rublev is in the Russian mob?" asked Beanie.

"I've heard rumors," said Irving, tipping his head back as he took a long gulp of his drink.

"From who?"

Wiping his mouth with the back of his hand, Irving reached forward and slammed the empty glass on the coffee table. "Look, I don't remember, okay? All I know is, Rublev is lying about me. I wasn't laundering money. Rublev was framing me and he convinced Saul to turn against me."

"And is that why you tried to kill Saul?" asked Beanie, even though he knew it was risky.

Irving scowled at him. "I didn't try to kill Saul."

"You were just rearranging his pillow?"

Shrugging, Irving looked away. "Believe me, or not. I don't care. Here's the truth—Rublev set me up."

"Why would Rublev want Saul to think you were laundering money?"

His stare intense, Irving said, "Rublev wanted to get me out of the way. He wanted me out of the company so he could take over. He wants to steal Saul's company. Give it to the Russian mob."

"And why would he do that?" asked Beanie, wondering if Irving had already had a few glasses of rum before he showed up.

"If anyone is laundering money, it's Rublev," insisted Irving, his eyes wide and wild.

Beanie cleared his throat. Irving was sticking to his unsubstantiated theory of Ivan Rublev as a mobster who set him up, which sounded ridiculous and like the ravings of a drunk.

Beanie said, "Let me ask you this: what do you know about Kenneth Moreaux?"

Irving frowned. "Why are you asking about Ken?"

"I heard he and Saul had some kind of falling out?" probed Beanie, deciding to be cagey, and not let Irving know about Tammy Biaggio's assertions against Kenneth Moreaux.

"Wasn't exactly a falling out," said Irving, eyebrows drawn together, expression concerned. "Ken suffered a mental breakdown."

Beanie scratched his chin. "Because of the car accident."

Slumping back on the couch, Irving said, "Ken lost his mind. After the car wreck, he initially seemed okay but it soon became very clear that he was no longer in possession of his faculties. That's why Saul had to dissolve their business partnership."

"Saul thought Moreaux was going crazy?"

Exhaling, Irving said, "He thought Ken was having a mental decline. Neurologically speaking. Saul believed Ken suffered a traumatic brain injury."

"What did you think?"

"Well, I wasn't as close to Ken as Saul was," said Irving. "I didn't work directly with him. But, from what Saul told me, in the months before they parted ways, Ken became very forgetful. He lost track of time. Disappeared for hours, sometimes days, and couldn't remember where he'd been. And Ken had violent mood swings. He would curse and lash out. He became physically violent."

"Physically violent?" repeated Beanie, recalling what Tammy Biaggio had told him about Moreaux beating his fists against the window of the Rolls Royce.

"I was in the office one morning when Ken smashed a vase and then lunged at the receptionist."

"Are you serious?"

Nodding, Irving said, "Saul had to keep Ken from going for her throat. I helped him get Ken out of there. It was painful for Saul to witness. He and Ken had been best friends since high school."

Filing away the information, Beanie said, "Listen, I'm sure I know the answer to this question, but I have to ask it. Is it possible that Kenneth Moreaux stabbed Saul?"

Quincy Irving scoffed. "Anything is possible. The real question is, is it probable? And, no, it isn't. I don't believe Ken would ever hurt Saul. But Ivan Rublev definitely would."

"Because Rublev wants Saul's company," guessed Beanie, not in the mood for more of Irving's drunken blame-shifting.

Irving leaned forward, his right eye twitching. "When you met with Rublev, did he seem upset about what happened to Saul?"

"I'm not really sure," said Beanie.

"Well, I can tell you that Rublev is hoping that Saul dies," said Irving. "Because if Saul lives, he'll be able to tell the cops what happened to him —that Ivan Rublev stabbed him."

"Quincy Irving told you that I stabbed Saul?" Ivan Rublev scowled and shook his head.

Sitting across from the Controller at Biaggio Loans, Inc., Beanie shifted in the chair on the opposite side of the man's large desk, which was messier than he'd expected. Files, documents, and errant slips of paper joined the writing pads, pens, and other odd bric-a-brac strewn across the gleaming surface. Rublev had a small interior office, with no windows, illuminated by fluorescent lighting that gave off a stark, artificial glow.

Following his meeting with Quincy Irving the day before, Beanie wasn't sure what to make of the disgruntled ex-CFO's bold claim. According to Irving, not only was Ivan Rublev working for the Russian mafia but the made man was also the person who'd stabbed Saul Biaggio.

Beanie wasn't about to put Irving's allegations in an article.

At least, not without talking to Ivan Rublev first. He'd returned to the *Palmchat Gazette* offices and made a call to the Controller, convincing the man to meet with him again to discuss what he promised would be a bombshell revelation.

When Beanie presented Ivan Rublev with Irving's wild assertion, the

Controller appeared shocked. Initially, he'd thought Beanie was joking. When informed that Irving had accused him of a crime, the shock turned to anger.

"That's ridiculous!" bellowed Rublev. "Why would I want to stab Saul?"

"Well, Quincy Irving has a theory," began Beanie, going on to tell Rublev about Irving's claim that he worked for the Russian mob, and wanted to steal Saul's business.

Scoffing, Rublev said, "So, my name is Rublev and that means I'm a Russian gangster?"

"Honestly, I think he was deflecting," said Beanie. "Shifting the blame back to you because he thinks you lied to Saul about him laundering money."

"I didn't lie to Saul," insisted Rublev. "Illegal funds are being laundered through this business."

"And you have definitive proof of that?"

Rublev sighed. "Not definitive proof, no. But Irving was the CFO. He's the only one who could have approved the movement of funds in a way they were transferred."

"Tell me this," said Beanie. "How did you begin to suspect the money laundering?"

With a sigh, Rublev said, "About four months ago, during my normal loan reconciliation duties, I noticed a large volume of clients making payments to the company, however, these clients did not seem to exist."

"The clients didn't exist?" Beanie shook his head. "I don't understand."

"They were dummy clients," said Rublev. "They weren't real. Just names in a database. And these fake clients had improvement loans for hundreds of thousands of dollars for houses in Handweg Gardens, amounts which far exceeded the value of the homes."

"Interesting," said Beanie, scratching his chin. Home values in Handweg Gardens, a marginalized, disenfranchised neighborhood had historically been economically depressed. Noelle's mom, who owned a small shotgun house in the neighborhood, often complained about the devaluation of her property, which was due to high crime rates and the lack of economic advancement.

Rublev said, "Furthermore, the homes didn't exist. They were just random addresses that led to nowhere. When I tried to locate them on the map, they couldn't be found."

"So the dummy clients and properties were used to hide the money laundering," said Beanie, understanding the scheme. At its simplest, money laundering was the process of making illegally obtained money, often from criminal activities, appear as if it came from legitimate sources—in other words, loan repayments.

Rublev nodded. "So, we have all these loans on the books that need to be repaid. And I find out the loans aren't real. But, we are receiving payments for them. Tens of thousands of dollars each month from people who, realistically, don't have tens of thousands of dollars. So how are they paying back these loans."

"Well, they're not because the customers aren't real and the houses don't exist."

"And yet, there is meticulous loan paperwork, with every 'I' dotted and every 'T' crossed, for each of these fake customers who don't exist," said Rublev. "And do you know who authorized each of these loans?"

"Quincy Irving," guessed Beanie.

"As the CFO, the way Saul has structured his business, Irving has the final authority on who receives a loan," said Rublev. "And so, he must be the money launderer. But, of course, he denies this when Saul confronts him. Says that someone must have forged his signature."

"Is that possible?" asked Beanie.

Rublev shook his head. "I doubt it. But, soon, I hope to have the proof I need to take my suspicions to the police."

"How will you get the proof?" asked Beanie.

Smiling like the goat who'd swallowed the grass, Rublev said, "I have spent the past month trying to follow the money trail. I have, so far, traced the loan repayments to a bank in the Cayman Islands. I have a friend who works there and I am hoping to call in a favor to find out the name associated with the numbered account."

"And you suspect that numbered account will be linked to Quincy Irving?"

"I am sure of it," said Rublev.

Beanie asked, "Do you think Irving is working for the Russian mob?"

"He's in bed with some sort of criminals," said Rublev. "And they are dangerous. One night, a few weeks ago, some guys beat him up."

"Irving told you that?"

Rublev shook his head. "Lisette happened to be with him at the time. She can tell the story better than I can. I'll buzz her and tell her to come to my office."

Fifteen minutes later, Lisette Javon, perched on the edge of the other chair in front of Rublev's desk, said, "Quincy and I were working late one night. When we left, Quincy walked me to my car. That's when three goons appeared and started walking toward us. The thugs looked like bad news, and Quincy immediately started to sweat. He looked petrified, not surprisingly. I was terrified, as well."

"And this was last month?" asked Beanie.

"Maybe two months ago," said Lisette. "Anyway, I wanted to call the police, but Quincy told me not to. I was confused, and he said he knew the men, and what they wanted. The thugs told me to leave, but I refused. I wasn't about to leave Quincy there alone. I didn't know what they might do to him. They looked like they would hurt him."

"Did they?" Beanie asked.

Shaking her head, Lisette said, "No, but they demanded to speak with him alone. So, Quincy told me that I should go home. He promised me he would be okay. I didn't want to leave him, but he insisted. For my protection. Because he didn't want anything bad to happen to me."

"And what did you do?"

"I'm ashamed to say that I left," Lisette said, hanging her head. "Because Quincy didn't come to work the next day, but when he did, two days later, he had a purplish bruise around his left eye."

"They must have beat him up," said Rublev. "My guess is there was some issue with the money laundering scheme and they wanted to keep him in line. Maybe he wanted out of the scam. Maybe he was skimming."

"When I asked Quincy about his eye, and if the thugs had hurt him," said Lisette, "he claimed he'd fallen trying to trim tree branches. He said the guys who'd approached us in the parking garage had the wrong person. But I didn't believe him. I think those goons were PC-5 members."

Beanie focused on her delicate frown. "Why do you think the guys were PC-5?"

Lisette's expression turned apprehensive. "Because as I was walking to my car, I heard one of them say they had a message from Nico Lecrae."

15

Back at his small desk in his tiny cubicle at the *Palmchat Gazette*, Beanie took a sip of what would most likely be his last cup of coffee of the day.

Following the meeting with Ivan Rublev and Lisette Javon, Beanie found himself consumed with thoughts about the PC-5 roughing up Quincy Irving at the request of Nico Lecrae.

At Lisette's mention of that name, Beanie had shuddered involuntarily.

Nico Lecrae was the head of the PC-5's St. Killian's operations. A scion of the founding cartel members, Lecrae was a ruthless mafia boss who orchestrated and directed the cartel's criminal operations across the world.

He had also been instrumental in saving Noelle's life.

Beanie didn't like to think that his wife owed the gang leader her existence, but if not for Lecrae's intervention, Ethan and Evan might be motherless children. Nevertheless, Beanie couldn't bring himself to be thankful for Lecrae. The man was a degenerate crook, a homicidal thug in a bespoke suit who pretended to be a gentleman, hobnobbing with the wealthy and fabulous. But the man's billions were as dirty as his hands, which were covered in blood from all the murder and mayhem caused by his violent enterprise.

Beanie tossed the empty Styrofoam cup into the trashcan under his desk.

If Lisette Javon had heard the goons mention Lecrae's name, then the PC-5 was definitely involved. But, had the island gang used Quincy Irving to help them launder filthy lucre? Beanie wasn't sure.

Drumming his hands on the desk, Beanie contemplated the possibility. If Irving was working for the island cartel, and they'd sent thugs to beat him up, why? Maybe Ivan's theories were right. Maybe Irving was skimming. Or had threatened to expose the scheme. Or had made some mistake, an accounting error perhaps, that jeopardized the scam.

Beanie leaned back in his chair.

He needed to find out more about the PC-5 threatening Quincy Irving.

And there was only one person who could give him that information.

Lime Shoes.

Half an hour later, Beanie took a quick sip of the Felipe beer he'd ordered while waiting for the old gangster to join him.

When Beanie arrived at the Purple Gecko, the seedy bar in Handweg Gardens where Lime Shoes held court, he'd been directed by two henchmen to wait at the gangster's table in the far corner. Beanie had sat in the booth many times before, and it always made him anxious, antsy. The table was too far from the door. Far from a quick escape, should anything crazy happen. If gunshots rang out, Beanie wasn't sure how he would make it to the exit without catching a bullet in the back.

He tried not to think about a gunfight at the Purple Gecko and focused on why he needed to talk to Lime Shoes. Staring at the shark's tooth on the chain around the old gangster's neck, Beanie couldn't help but think of the rumor that Lime Shoes had killed a shark that had tried to attack him and snatched out the beast's teeth. An interesting yarn, but who knew if it was true.

"Who told you that the PC-5 gave Quincy Irving a warning?" asked Lime Shoes after Beanie recounted the story Lisette Javon had told him about PC-5 goons beating up the former CFO of Biaggio Loans, Inc.

Beanie cleared his throat, and answered, "I'd rather not say."

Lime Shoes took a sip of his whisky. "Why am I not surprised?"

"Is it true?" asked Beanie.

"Why did this person tell you that the cartel warned Irving?" asked Lime Shoes.

Wary of inciting the old gangster's ire, Beanie said, "Well, they seem to think that Irving is working with the gang. Laundering money for the cartel. For Nico Lecrae."

"Lecrae doesn't use outsiders to launder his money," said Lime Shoes. "Everything is done in-house. For safety reasons."

Beanie nodded. It made sense that Lecrae wouldn't trust any criminal organization other than his own to clean his dirty funds. As Beanie understood it, Lecrae's illegal cash was laundered by a separate faction of the PC-5, but Beanie didn't want to understand it. Best not to know too much about the details and inner workings of the island cartel. Knowledge was not power. It was dangerous.

Beanie took a sip of beer, though he was no longer interested in nursing the island brew. "Is it possible Irving could have been laundering money for Russian mobsters? And maybe Lecrae found out and got upset?"

Shaking his head, Lime Shoes said, "Mr. Lecrae wouldn't care. That would be small potatoes. Not even on his radar."

"I see," said Beanie.

"However," said Lime Shoes, "if Irving is laundering money for some Russians, then it could be possible that Irving didn't pay his protection tax. You want to do something illegal in a certain area of town. Fine. But you have to get permission. And permission ain't cheap."

"Permission costs," said Beanie. "Meaning, Irving would have to pay a fee?"

"Pay to play," confirmed Lime Shoes. "You pay permission. And you pay a percentage of your profits."

"I see," said Beanie, thinking that whoever said crime doesn't pay must not have heard of the PC-5. The island cartel made a pretty penny in protection taxes. After all, what was permission if not protection from the cartel's wrath, which a person would incur if they set up shop without making sure it was okay to do so?

"But my source said Lecrae's name was mentioned as the person with a message for Quincy Irving," said Beanie.

Lime Shoes shrugged. "Sometimes, the street boss will invoke the big boss's name to get a point across. Mr. Lecrae doesn't mind that if it will help resolve issues."

Understanding, Beanie nodded. "So, the street boss had a problem with Irving."

"He might have if Irving wasn't paying his protection tax," said Lime Shoes, after another quick sip of the dark liquid in his glass. "But, Quincy Irving didn't need to pay protection tax because the man wasn't laundering money for the Russians. Whoever told you that was misinformed."

"So, Biaggio Loans, Inc. is not being used to launder money for Russians?" asked Beanie.

Lime Shoes scratched the scraggly gray hairs clinging to his chin. "Here's the deal. Biaggio Loans, Inc. is being used to launder cash for a Russian gangster. But, as I said, Quincy Irving isn't in bed with the Russians."

"Then who is?" asked Beanie, wondering if Irving had been telling the truth about Ivan Rublev.

"That I don't know," admitted Lime Shoes.

Tempering his frustration, Beanie asked, "Okay, tell me this: If Irving wasn't laundering money, then why would the PC-5 guys beat him up?"

"Because Irving wasn't paying his gambling debts."

Floored, Beanie stared at the old gangster. "Gambling debts?"

"Quincy Irving got roughed up because the man is hundreds of thousands of dollars in the hole," said Lime Shoes. "He's addicted to the blackjack table."

16

"So, if Lime Shoes was telling the truth, and he had no reason to lie to me, then Quincy Irving isn't laundering money for the Russians," said Beanie, staring at the coffee in his Styrofoam cup, made ten minutes ago, when he'd joined his coworkers Caleb and Stevie in the breakroom for an impromptu speculation session regarding the Biaggio case. As they drank their respective libations, Beanie brought the guys up to date with the latest information, including details of his conversations with the Biaggio Loans employees and Lime Shoes.

Caleb harrumphed. "I don't think you can jump to that conclusion just yet."

"But Lime Shoes would know who's laundering money at Biaggio Loans, right?" asked Stevie.

Beanie took a sip of coffee. "That's the problem, though. Lime Shoes didn't know. He confirmed that someone is laundering money at the company, but he couldn't give me the name of the person working with the Russians."

"Which means that he doesn't know for sure that it's not Quincy Irving," pointed out Caleb. "Irving could have covered his tracks very well."

"That's certainly possible," Beanie acknowledged.

"And it actually makes sense that Quincy Irving is the money launderer," continued Caleb. "If the man has gambling debts, and the PC-5 is threatening to break his kneecaps, then he needs money to pay his debts. What better way to do that than to work for Russian gangsters, who most likely take care of Irving's debts in exchange for the laundry services."

"And Irving did try to finish Saul off in the hospital," reminded Stevie. "Think about it. If Irving loses his job, he loses his ability to launder money for the Russians. With Saul dead, Irving might have thought he could keep his job. Maybe even take over the company."

Beanie said, "Well, Irving said Rublev is trying to take over the company so he could use it as a front for money laundering. And that's possible, as well. Rublev would need to get Quincy Irving out of the way. Irving might have discovered that Rublev was laundering money, so Rublev went on the offensive and framed Irving, spreading lies about Irving to Saul, who believed the lies and fired Irving."

"I still think Quincy Irving is the money launderer," said Stevie.

"Me, too," said Caleb. "I know you trust Lime Shoes, but if Irving isn't guilty, then why did he try to kill Saul in the ICU? And nobody believes that goat wash about him rearranging Saul's pillow."

Beanie stroked his chin. "Yeah, but ..."

"What do you mean, but?" demanded Caleb. "Ivan Rublev doesn't even have a motive to want Saul dead."

"Well, Rublev has a motive if you believe Quincy Irving," said Stevie. "Which I don't."

Caleb said, "Okay, how about this: Have you considered Saul Biaggio?"

"What do you mean?" asked Beanie.

"What if Saul Biaggio is the money launderer?" proposed Caleb.

"That's something to think about," said Stevie.

Beanie was reluctant to embrace that conclusion. "I don't know ..."

"What don't you know?" asked Caleb. "Makes sense to me. Saul starts working for the Russians. Things are going fine until they aren't. I think Saul ran afoul of the mob and they sent him a message."

Sighing, Beanie sat back in his chair. "Seems like a mixed message to me."

"What do you mean?" asked Stevie.

"Let's say you're right, Caleb," said Beanie. "Saul is in bed with the Russians, then for whatever reason, things go sideways. So then the Russians send a henchman to stab Saul and leave him to die in Oyster Farms at the rental home of his ex-partner?"

"I don't think Saul was stabbed in Oyster Farms," said Stevie.

Caleb said, "I don't even think the henchmen deliberately chose Oyster Farms. I think they just dropped him off on the street and it happened to be in your neighborhood."

"Makes sense to me," said Stevie, nodding.

Beanie finished his coffee. "I don't know. There are still too many unknowns …"

Twenty minutes later, back at his small desk in his tiny cubicle, Beanie picked up the ringing phone.

"Hey, it's Fields," said the officer. "Wanted to give you the latest on the Biaggio case."

"What happened?" asked Beanie, turning to his computer to open a Word document.

Fields said, "Saul's Rolls Royce was recovered yesterday."

"What?" Beanie was confused. "I didn't know it was missing."

"Remember when I told you that Tammy Biaggio was cleared as a suspect by Janvier," said Fields. "And I didn't know how at the time."

"You figured it was some home surveillance showing she couldn't have stabbed Saul."

"Well, I was right," Fields said. "Turns out, after leaving their New Year's Eve party, Saul and Tammy arrived at their mansion in Avalon Estates at 2:46 a.m., according to their exterior surveillance. Their interior surveillance and alarm system shows they entered their home at 2:52 a.m."

Grabbing a sticky pad, Beanie scribbled the times Fields told him. "So, probably took them six or seven minutes to get out of the car and into the house."

"Right," confirmed Fields. "But, then the interior surveillance shows Saul – alone, by himself – leaving the house at 3:37 a.m."

"Why did Saul leave the house at 3:37 in the morning?"

"That's the question no one has the answer to," said Fields. "When Janvier questioned Tammy Biaggio, she said she didn't even realize Saul had left the house."

"Right," said Beanie, recalling what Tammy had told him.

The only thing I know is I went to bed with my husband and I woke up to the police at my door telling me Saul had been stabbed, then taken to the hospital, went through emergency surgery, and was placed in a medically induced coma.

"Then the Rolls is seen backing out of the driveway at 3:39 a.m.," said Fields. "And that seems to be the last time the Rolls was seen, although Janvier is reviewing CCTV footage during the time between three am and six in the morning."

"So, sometime between around three-forty and six a.m. is when Saul was stabbed," said Beanie, typing the notes into his document.

Fields said, "So, the Rolls was found when the car was pulled over during a routine traffic violation stop and the officer got information that the plates didn't match the vehicle. The VIN number showed the car was a Rolls Royce owned by Saul Biaggio."

"Who was driving the car?"

"Don't know the name off the top of my head," said Fields. "But the driver claims he bought the car from a used luxury car lot and swore the owner told him the title was clear."

"Is Janvier planning to talk to the car lot owner?"

"Not sure," said Fields. "Janvier is still focused on Quincy Irving as the guy who stabbed Saul, despite the lack of any evidence tying to man to the crime."

"Well, Irving might have a motive."

"Yeah, I know," said Fields. "Money laundering. Ivan Rublev told Janvier that, but Rublev has no proof. Despite that, Janvier is running with the theory because the nurse claims Irving tried to suffocate Saul with a pillow."

"So, Janvier thinks Irving wanted Saul dead because Saul fired him," said Beanie, finding it interesting that his coworkers agreed with the misguided detective.

"And, also turns out that Quincy Irving doesn't seem to have an alibi for the night that Saul was stabbed," said Fields. "According to Irving's wife, she thought he was out of town, which obviously was a lie."

Beanie sat back in his chair. "So where was Quincy Irving that night?"

Fields said, "So far, that's a question the man refuses to answer."

17

"And I just don't think it's a good idea, you know?"

Staring at the ceiling fan above the queen-sized bed in the master bedroom, Beanie settled against the pillows stacked in front of the headboard.

"You don't think what's a good idea?" he asked.

Noelle stopped at the foot of the bed to stare at him. "Were you listening?"

Sheepish, Beanie said, "Sort of … "

The truth was, he'd been thinking about the Biaggio case, ruminating over what he'd learned so far, wondering why Saul Biaggio had left his house at three in the morning. Where had the man been going? Possibly to meet someone. But who? The Russian gangsters? Beanie contemplated Caleb's theory. It hadn't occurred to him that Saul Biaggio might be a crook. But what if he was and the Russians had demanded his presence at an early morning meeting? What if Saul and the Russians had disagreed about something and Saul had been stabbed? Possible, but still, how had Saul ended up at Kenneth Moreaux's rental property in Oyster Farms?

Exhaling, his wife tossed one of her hair ties at him. Beanie laughed and twisted his body to avoid being hit, allowing the object to land somewhere between the pillows behind him.

"I was telling you that Amber wants to introduce Damon to her father," said Noelle. "And I told her I didn't think that was a good idea. We had a disagreement and now I think she's upset with me, but she asked me what I thought. I can't imagine the point of Lime Shoes and Damon sitting down to dinner with each other."

"I can't imagine the point of Amber and Fields," said Beanie, closing his eyes.

"What does that mean?"

Picking up on the ice in his wife's demand, Beanie opened his eyes, not surprised to find her scowling at him as she slathered her legs with body butter.

"Babe, you know I don't like the idea of Fields and Amber."

"But I don't know why," said Noelle, lowering her right leg to the floor and lifting her left leg onto the settee so she could smooth the body butter over her smooth skin. "Amber is pretty and sweet and—"

"And her father is Lime Shoes."

"So what?" demanded Noelle. "Her father's a gangster so she doesn't deserve love?"

"That's not what I said, or meant," said Beanie. "And you have a problem with her father, too."

"I have a problem with her introducing her father to her new boyfriend," clarified Noelle, strolling through the entryway into the en suite bathroom.

Beanie pinched the bridge of his nose. The last thing he wanted was to discuss the love life of two consenting adults who, ultimately, would make decisions that best suited their lives regardless of what anyone thought. He especially didn't want to have the conversation because he suspected it might lead to an argument, or at least a heated discussion he didn't want to engage in when he just wanted to sleep.

Coming out of the bathroom, Noelle said, "I mean, imagine if I asked you to meet my father."

"You would never do that," said Beanie.

Noelle walked to the wardrobe, opened it, and replaced the colorful kimono she'd donned after her shower.

"I know that," said his wife. "But imagine if I did."

"Then I'd meet him."

Noelle faced him, then marched toward the bed. "Wait. You want to meet my father?"

"That's not what I said …"

"But do you want to meet him?"

"I wouldn't say that I want to meet him," said Beanie, knowing he had to tread both lightly and carefully to avoid an explosion. "It's not on my bucket list, or anything but …"

"But?"

"But, if you wanted me to meet him, then I wouldn't be averse to that."

Pivoting, Noelle walked around the bed to the other side, where she slept. "Well, I'm never going to want you to meet him."

"Why not?" asked Beanie, though he doubted his wife would elaborate. She'd always been vague, evasive, and downright secretive when it came to details about her father.

"Do you really have to ask me that?" Noelle shook her head. "The man is a cold-blooded killer."

"I know that—"

"Don't you have enough murderers in your life?"

"What?"

"You're the journalist who is always part of the stories he covers, right?" Noelle shook her head as she slipped beneath the covers. "You're always coming face to face with a killer."

"No, I'm not," protested Beanie.

Noelle moved closer until she was in his arms. "Yes, you are. Would you like me to remind you?"

Kissing the top of his wife's head, Beanie chuckled. "Not really."

"I know it's the brand that you're cultivating," said Noelle. "And people really like your stories. You're getting popular and I do love that for you, but just do me a favor, okay?"

"Anything," promised Beanie.

"Don't get yourself killed," said his wife. "The boys like having you around and I think you're okay, too."

"Awww, Elle, you like me," teased Beanie.

"Yes, I do, and that reminds me," said his wife.

"What?"

"You remember my cousin Kelly, right?"

"Kelly? Yeah … " said Beanie, struggling to remember who his wife was talking about. "How's she doing?"

"You don't remember," said Noelle, giggling as she slapped his arm.

"Okay, so I don't …" admitted Beanie, sheepish.

"Anyway," continued Noelle. "Well, Kelly's boyfriend, Umar, works at the Queen Palm, and he was on duty the night of the Biaggio New Year's party. He was working as a men's room attendant at the event."

"Interesting …"

"I thought you would think so," said Noelle. "So, Kelly says Umar, along with all the other hotel employees, were questioned by the police about the Biaggio party, considering what happened to Saul."

"What did the cops ask the hotel employees?"

"Kelly isn't sure," said Noelle. "All she knows is Umar lied to the police."

"Why did he lie to the cops?"

"Apparently, Umar lied because he was paid to stay quiet about some incident he saw in the men's restroom."

"Wonder what he saw?"

"You can find out," said Noelle. "Umar is willing to give you the story if you help him deal with coming clean to the cops."

18

Surrounded by a circle of twelve-foot bottle palm trees, named for their swollen gray trunks, which looked like bottles spouting arched, glossy dark fronds, the valet station at the Queen Palm Resort & Casino was somewhat deserted at three in the afternoon.

Beanie had hoped that would be the case when he'd decided a visit Umar Phillips, the boyfriend of Noelle's cousin Kelly. Flight schedules being as they were, Beanie knew that most tourists arrived on the island in the early morning or late afternoon, which was when the hotel was probably busiest.

A hotel employee, dressed in a pale green short-sleeved polo shirt and khaki shorts, stood beneath a portico in front of a row of French doors that opened to a vestibule leading to the hotel's three-story garage. The valet, a laconic kid with close-cropped hair, leaned against a podium, one eye on his phone.

As Beanie approached him, heading beneath the portico, the laconic kid glanced at him, and shoved his phone into his pocket.

"You need your car, sir?" asked the laconic kid, whose small mother-of-pearl nameplate said KENNY.

"Actually," said Beanie, thankful for the portico's shade, and the errant ocean-scented breeze. "I was hoping to talk to Umar Phillips."

"Umar?" asked Kenny. "He's in the back. I'll get him for you."

As Kenny hurried off, Beanie considered his wife's request to help her cousin's boyfriend in exchange for information. Beanie had immediately agreed. He wanted to know what the hotel employee had seen in the men's room. What was the mysterious incident he'd been paid to stay quiet about? Who had paid him? And why? Considering that the incident had occurred at the Biaggio's party, Beanie wondered if it might have something to do with Saul Biaggio's stabbing, though he couldn't imagine how. Quincy Irving, the main suspect, had been disinvited from the shindig. And Saul had been attacked long after the party was over.

"Mr. Bean ..."

Hearing his name, Beanie turned. A tall, lanky islander with a bald head and an anxious expression hurried toward him. After introducing himself, Beanie said, "Kelly, my wife's cousin, said you wanted to speak about something that occurred on New Year's Eve."

Nodding, Umar said, "Let's talk over here."

Beanie followed the hotel employee to a picturesque outdoor sitting area several feet from the valet station, a waiting area with stone benches surrounded by hibiscus bushes and Sego palm trees.

After they sat on one of the benches, Umar said, "I was a fool to lie to the cops."

"Why did you?" asked Beanie, interested in hearing the story from the man's own words, though he was aware that Umar had been paid for his silence.

Shaking his head, Umar said, "Stupid mistake. But the money was good. Way more than I'd made in tips the whole night and I'd made some pretty good tip money. Anyway, when the cops asked me if I had seen anything strange or suspicious or anything that seemed off during the Biaggio party, I told them no."

"But that wasn't the truth?"

Umar exhaled. "No. I definitely saw something strange, suspicious, and off."

Intrigued, Beanie asked, "Kelly said something happened in the men's room. Can you tell me about it?"

"I was assigned the men's bathroom for the party," began Umar. "Wasn't excited about that. Tips are okay, but guys don't go to the bathroom like women do, you know? So there's long stretches of time when nobody's in there. And, anyway, I'm a sociable guy so I like to be in the dining room, mingling with the people, you know?"

"Right," said Beanie, eager for the man to get to the point, but willing to be patient with him.

"So, I'm in the men's room during a lull in the action," said Umar. "I'm doing my duties. Wiping down the sinks. Cleaning the mirrors. The floors. Basic duties. Next thing I know, Saul Biaggio comes into the men's room."

"Saul came into the men's room?" Beanie was shocked, though he supposed he shouldn't be since Saul had to relieve himself just like anyone else.

"But he wasn't alone," said Umar. "I was near the last stall when Saul and the other guy came in. Saul was telling the guy to calm down, but the guy was crazy mad. I mean livid. Steaming with rage. He was cursing up a storm. Calling Saul every name in the book. And I thought Saul was going to knock him out, but the man was so calm. He was talking to the guy. Telling him to calm down. Telling him everything was going to be okay."

"You have any idea what the guy was mad about?"

"None whatsoever," said Umar. "But the guy was mad, he said Saul was an evil crook."

"Evil crook …" echoed Beanie, finding something vaguely familiar about the insult.

"And then the man told Saul he would kill him," said Umar.

"Are you serious?"

"Said he would put a stake in Saul's heart because he was a vampire," said Umar, eyes wide as the memory of what he'd witnessed no doubt replayed in his mind. "I was so scared. I didn't know what to think. Maybe the man was drunk. Or crazy. Off his meds, you know?"

Beanie said, "And then what happened?"

"It was the most odd thing," said Umar. "After all that cursing and threatening to kill Saul, the man went rigid, and I mean absolutely still, and I thought he was having a seizure. But, then he collapsed to the ground and started to weep like a child."

"What did Saul do?"

"He got on his knees next to the man," said Umar. "He put an arm around him and told him to calm down and things would be okay. It was at that time that Saul looked up at me. He said to me, you never saw this, understand? And he took out his wallet and tossed it to me. He told me to take all of the cash inside of the wallet and keep my mouth shut. It was eighteen hundred dollars. There wasn't even a fourth of that amount in my tip bowl! So, I took the money. And then Saul told me to leave the restroom and put an out-of-order sign on the door so no one would come in."

"And you did that?"

His expression pained, Umar nodded. "I know I shouldn't have. I feel horrible. I couldn't even spend the money, especially when I found out that Saul Biaggio got stabbed. I kept thinking to myself that the man who cursed him and promised to kill him actually tried to do it. The man said he would put a knife in Saul Biaggio and he did. And I just think if I don't say anything, the man is going to get away with it."

Beanie exhaled, struggling to process what Umar had told him. "You do need to go to the police."

"I know, but I'm scared," said Umar. "What if I get in trouble for lying? I want to do the right thing but I don't want to get arrested."

"Listen, I have a friend who's a police officer," said Beanie. "I'll contact him. Tell him you want to speak with the police. He'll be able to help you."

"Thank you," whispered Umar, hanging his head.

"I think it'll be okay," said Beanie, gently clapping the man's shoulder. "I'm sure the police will ask you to describe the man who threatened Saul. You remember what he looks like?"

"I think so," said Umar. "But, I know his name."

Shocked, Beanie said, "You do?"

Umar nodded. "When Saul was trying to get the man to calm down, he said to the man, 'it's going to be alright. Don't worry, Ken ..."

19

"Janvier took Umar Phillip's statement," said Officer Damon Fields when Beanie called him for an update on the Biaggio case. "But I'm not sure what he thinks about it."

"You're kidding?" Leaning back in the chair in his small cubicle at the *Palmchat Gazette* offices, Beanie was astonished, though he figured he shouldn't have been. Janvier had never been one to carefully consider the clues right in front of him. He held tightly to his confirmation biases, whether they made sense, or not.

Two days ago, when Beanie spoke with Umar Phillips, and learned the details of the incident that had occurred in the men's room at the Biaggio New Year's Eve party, he'd left the hotel and called Fields. After relaying Phillips' story, Fields agreed to meet with the man and facilitate a meeting with Detective Janvier.

"Shouldn't Janvier be questioning Kenneth Moreaux?" asked Beanie. "It's obvious that Moreaux threatened Saul in the men's room."

"I think so, too," said Fields.

"And Moreaux has a motive," said Beanie. "You know, he started acting violent after his car accident. He sued Saul for kicking him out of the company. And when I talked to Tammy Biaggio, she told me that Moreaux forced her and Saul off the road."

"I think that's what she told Janvier, as well," said Fields. "And Janvier told her that was no proof of her story, but he would look into it. That's the same thing he told Umar Phillips. There's no proof that what Umar said is true. He's the only witness. Saul is in a coma so he can't corroborate Umar's story."

"Which is why Janvier needs to talk to Moreaux," said Beanie.

"Listen, man, I agree," said Fields. "Especially in light of these new developments."

"New developments?" Beanie pulled his chair closer to his computer and opened a Word document.

"So, I told you Janvier was reviewing CCTV footage, right? Well, after the Biaggio party ended, CCTV cameras in downtown St. Killian show Saul's Rolls Royce being pursued at a high rate of speed by a black Mercedes."

"Was the license plate visible on the Mercedes?"

"The black Mercedes is registered to Kenneth Moreaux," said Fields. "And on one camera angle, you can clearly see him driving the car."

"That lines up with Tammy Biaggio's story," said Beanie.

"Possibly," said Fields. "The problem is, Saul turns onto a side street. Moreaux follows, and at that point, they're driving into the heart of downtown where there are either no cameras or cameras that don't work, because we have no footage of the two cars driving through downtown."

Beanie sighed. "So, no footage of Moreaux forcing Saul off the road."

"Right," said Fields. "However, there is CCTV of Kenneth Moreaux's Mercedes at a gas station. The Island Gas & Go. Moreaux gets out of his car and goes inside the station mart."

"Did Janvier talk to the clerk?"

"He did, but I don't have any details yet," said Fields. "Listen, dispatch is calling me. I'll give you a call if I get more details."

"Thanks," said Beanie, hanging up the phone. As he finished typing notes, he concluded that waiting for Janvier to reveal information to Fields was probably a long shot. His best bet was to talk to the gas station clerk himself.

An hour or so later, Beanie walked into the Island Gas & Go. The young West Indian girl behind the counter directed Beanie to the candy and chip aisle, in the center of the convenience mart, where her coworker, the clerk who'd been on duty when Moreaux visited the mart, was restocking bars of chocolate and bags of plantain crisps.

"Thanks for talking to me," said Beanie, after introducing himself to the clerk, a thin thirtysomething man with tan skin and wispy hair combed over his bald pate.

"No problem, man," said the clerk, sitting on an overturned plastic crate, reaching down to grab candy bars from a cardboard box positioned between his feet. "I want to know what's going on. Figure we can share information."

"Share information?"

"That old dude is in big trouble, huh?" asked the clerk, a curious glee in his dark gaze. "The cops wouldn't tell me nothing but they came here asking about him, so I figure he must have done something bad."

"The police believe so," said Beanie.

"What did he do?" The clerk lined chocolate bars in a basket tray on a shelf. "Put hands on his old lady?"

"The police think he assaulted someone," said Beanie.

"Figures," said the clerk. "I knew that old dude was bad news as soon as he walked through the door."

"Why do you say that?"

"Because he comes in and says he needs the bathroom," said the clerk. "But he looks nervous and crazy. He's in a nice suit, though. So I figured he was at some fancy New Year's party. But, I'm thinking he must have got into a fight because he's got blood on the front of his shirt."

"Blood?"

The clerk nodded as he reached down into the cardboard box for more candy bars. "So he goes in the bathroom and he's in there for a while. I'm getting nervous, you know. Is the old dude puking all over the place? Bleeding out? Finally, he comes out and the front of his shirt is wet, and I can tell he tried to wash the blood out because the shirt looks like he took it off and put it back on. It's not buttoned right, you know? So I ask him if everything is okay. He gives me a dirty look, then says yeah. I ask him if he got something on his shirt. He says red wine, then just walks out. Doesn't even buy anything. Walks out to his Mercedes, gets in, and then speeds off."

Interesting, thought Beanie, scratching his chin.

"But, it's like I told that cop," said the clerk. "I know what a red wine stain looks like and I know what a bloodstain looks like. And that was blood on his shirt."

20

"Quincy Irving is no longer a suspect," announced Vivian Thomas-Bronson, the editor of the *Palmchat Gazette*, a formidable foreign war correspondent who possessed beauty, brains, and a cutthroat approach to journalism, ensuring that the paper was always first to break a big story.

And Detective Janvier dropping the charges against his main suspect was a huge story with far-reaching consequences.

"Are you serious?" asked Beanie, taking a sip of his first cup of coffee of the day.

He'd just made the java and returned to his tiny cubicle to start the morning's tasks when Vivian called him to her office.

"I just spoke with my sources," said Vivian, turning to her computer.

"What did you find out?" asked Beanie, vaguely wondering about the identity of her source at the St. Killian police department. She'd never revealed the person or even given the barest hint at who it might be, though Beanie suspected it was Detective Baxter François, one of the famed François detectives, a quintet of brothers who were clever and cunning.

Detective François and Vivian had worked together on a dangerous case once, and Beanie surmised that a bond between them had been formed.

"Apparently," said Vivian, her fingers flying over the keyboard as she multi-tasked, checking emails as she talked with him. "Irving has an alibi for the night Saul was stabbed."

"Interesting," said Beanie, stroking his chin. "Last time I talked to Fields, he said Irving refused to tell the police where he was on the night in question."

"Well, there's a reason for that," said Vivian, glancing at him, her mouth twisted in a wry smirk. "Irving didn't want to tell the police that on New Year's Eve, he was at a low-rent casino in Little Turkey."

"That actually makes sense," said Beanie, reminding Vivian that Lime Shoes had revealed Quincy Irving's gambling problem.

"Video surveillance showed Irving entering the casino around eleven p.m.," said Vivian, focusing on her emails again. "He didn't leave until around seven a.m. the next morning."

After another sip of coffee, Beanie said, "From the camera surveillance and CCTV footage Janvier reviewed, the cops determined Saul was stabbed between three-thirty and six a.m."

"Which means Irving couldn't have stabbed Saul," said Vivian. "The casino may be in Little Turkey but the security is robust. There's no way Irving could have sneaked out of the place without being caught on camera."

Beanie shook his head. "I don't understand that guy. Why not just tell the police that from the beginning? He might have avoided the charges."

"Well, the attempted murder for his stunt in the ICU is still standing, for now," said Vivian. "But my source thinks that will be dropped, too, because the evidence is circumstantial and inconclusive. Did the nurse really see Irving trying to smother Saul or did she think that's what she saw?"

"Right," said Beanie, though he personally thought the ICU attempted murder should stick.

Vivian said, "Anyway, Irving was reluctant to reveal his alibi because he walked out of the casino stumbling and hungover with two scantily clad women draped all over him."

Scoffing, Beanie said, "No wonder he stayed quiet."

"He might as well have come clean," said Vivian. "In the end, his wife found out and I'm pretty sure his marriage is over."

Standing, Beanie said, "I think his marriage was over long before he walked into that casino."

Ten minutes later, back at his tiny desk, Beanie turned to his computer and opened a Word document. As he started his first draft for the new developments regarding Quincy Irving, Beanie wondered what could make a marriage collapse to the point where a man found himself gambling away all of his hard-earned money and partying with women other than his wife.

He wasn't sure and didn't want to know.

Beanie couldn't imagine his life without Noelle, and couldn't fathom breaking his vows, cheating, and keeping secrets. Although, Noelle had kept secrets from him. Huge secrets that made him question his marriage. But they'd gotten past it, thank goodness. They were stronger now, their union solidified, and whatever hardships, difficulties, or challenges lay ahead, he was confident they would face them together. They were partners for life, their union unbreakable.

Focusing on his computer, Beanie tested a few headlines. He wanted something intriguing and interesting, but he strove for integrity in his headlines. Some journalists employed click-bait techniques, but—

His desk phone rang.

"Roland Bean."

"Hey, it's Fields," said the officer. "I'm on break and figured I'd call because there have been developments."

"You talking about Quincy Irving?"

"How'd you now?" asked Fields.

"Vivian has a source," said Beanie.

"Does she, now," said Fields. "Who is it? François?"

"That's my guess, but she won't say," said Beanie. "Anything else going on?"

"Hey, you remember that diamond necklace you found in the backyard of Moreaux's rental property?" asked Fields.

His interest excited, Beanie asked, "Does it have something to do with Saul's stabbing?"

"Janvier doesn't think so," said Fields. "But, I wanted to mention it because he was livid that his CSI team didn't find it, and you did."

Beanie chuckled, though he was disappointed he hadn't found a viable clue.

"Janvier said the necklace could have been left there by the last family who rented the house."

"Yeah, agreed," admitted Beanie.

"Oh, and before I go, here's something that I should have led with," said Fields, who had a penchant for revealing bombshell revelations at the wrong time. "Janvier arrested a new suspect in the stabbing attack on Saul Biaggio."

"Yeah, you should have led with that," huffed Beanie. "Who is it?"

"Kenneth Moreaux."

21

"So, Detective Janvier arrested Kenneth Moreaux," said Stevie, taking a sip of his bottled water.

"That's a shame," said Caleb, shaking his head, bringing his mug of tea to his lips.

Halfway through his second cup of coffee of the day, Beanie nodded. "Yeah, I was shocked, too, but the evidence against Moreaux is pretty compelling."

At two in the afternoon, following lunch at his favorite food truck in Pourciau Square, Beanie joined his coworkers in the breakroom for an impromptu speculation session regarding their current stories.

Stevie started off the conversation with his story about another protest in Little Turkey, this time about a dangerous intersection where dozens of accidents, many of them fatal, had occurred. Residents were demanding a traffic light, while local civic leaders accused St. Killian's mayor of ignoring the impoverished neighborhood.

Then Caleb followed, grousing and grumbling about covering a society fundraiser benefitting the homeless, which he claimed the island's elite didn't really care about. "They just like to dress up, drink too much, and brag about how much money they have."

Finally, Beanie shared the latest developments in the Saul Biaggio stabbing case. After his conversation with Officer Fields and a quick consultation with Vivian, Beanie had written the first draft of EX-PARTNER ARRESTED IN BIAGGIO ATTACK.

"Until Fields called me today," began Beanie, "the last information I had was that he was seen at an Island Gas & Go."

"And you talked to the station clerk, and he told you about the stains on Moreaux's shirt," said Caleb, frowning. "Yeah, we know that. Get to the new information."

Tempering his annoyance, Beanie said, "Well, when Moreaux left the gas station, he drove home and was seen entering his garage on his exterior surveillance."

Caleb said, "Well, that puts the man in his house before Saul Biaggio was stabbed, right? So, how could he have done it?"

Beanie said, "Twenty minutes later, the Mercedes backs out of the garage."

"That's how he could have done it," said Stevie.

"There's no CCTV to show where Moreaux went," said Beanie. "However, his Mercedes has GPS and that system tracked the Mercedes to a seedy motel in Little Turkey called the Seahorse Inn."

"What happened at the motel?" asked Stevie. "Any idea why Moreaux went there?"

Beanie sighed. "So, here's where things get interesting. Remember Fields told me that Saul Biaggio left his house around three in the morning? Well, based on the GPS in the Rolls, Saul drove to the same seedy motel that Moreaux drove to, arriving about ten minutes after Moreaux showed up."

Caleb said, "Which means that Saul Biaggio left his house to meet Moreaux at the motel in Little Turkey."

"That's what I'm thinking," said Beanie. "Janvier feels the same way, considering that a burner phone was located in Moreaux's Mercedes, which the cops impounded and searched. Only one call was made from the burner and that call was made to Saul Biaggio."

"That's proof that Moreaux called Saul," said Stevie.

"Right," Beanie agreed. "So, a few hours later, the Mercedes left the motel."

"Where did Moreaux go?"

"Again, it gets very interesting," said Beanie. "Moreaux drove to his rental house in Oyster Farms. The Rolls remained at the motel."

Caleb said, "Which means Moreaux and Saul went to the rent house in Moreaux's Mercedes."

"But why?" asked Stevie. "And what's the deal with going to the motel?"

"I don't know," said Beanie. "It's weird. Anyway, the Mercedes leaves the rental house around five in the morning."

"That's when Saul jumped the fence into your backyard," said Caleb.

"Around that time," confirmed Beanie.

Stevie said. "Now I see why Janvier arrested Moreaux."

Nodding, Caleb said, "And the man has motive. He couldn't stand Saul for kicking him out of the business they built together."

"Yeah, but there's still some odd things that don't seem to have a good explanation," said Beanie. "Like, for instance, Saul's Rolls left the motel at seven am the next morning and drove to a used car lot."

"If Saul was bleeding from a stab wound," began Stevie, "then how could he have driven his Rolls to the car lot."

"Actually, Saul was in emergency surgery at seven that morning," said Beanie. "But, I agree. So, who drove the Rolls to the car lot? So, far, Janvier doesn't know because he hasn't spoken with the used car lot owner."

"Why not?"

"He's got his prime suspect," said Beanie. "As far as he's concerned, at this moment, Moreaux stabbed Saul. The burner phone wasn't the only evidence found in the Mercedes. Saul Biaggio's blood was found in the backseat."

"In the backseat?" asked Caleb. "Did Moreaux put Saul in the backseat of his car?"

Beanie said, "Fields told me that's another unexplained issue. But Janvier surmises that Moreaux stabbed Saul and the motel, put him in the backseat, then drove him to his rental house."

"That's weird," said Stevie. "Why would Moreaux take Saul to a location that's connected to him? He had to know the cops would look at him suspiciously."

"Janvier thinks Moreaux's current mental decline, due to the accident," said Beanie, "caused him to make irrational decisions."

"If Moreaux was operating with sound faculties," said Caleb. "Then he might not have stabbed Saul in the first place."

Beanie nodded. "But, as it stands, Moreaux has motive, opportunity, and he's got means."

"Means?" asked Stevie.

Beanie said, "The police found the knife used to stab Saul Biaggio in the Mercedes. It belongs to Kenneth Moreaux."

22

"I don't have water, tea, or coffee," groused Kenneth Moreaux as he made his way behind a large mahogany desk and dropped into a large leather chair, which creaked beneath his weight. "So, if you're thirsty, you're out of luck."

"Actually, I'm fine," said Beanie, not wanting to prolong the conversation with small talk and libations. "As I said, I just want to ask you a few questions and be on my way."

"You could have called," grumbled Moreaux, reaching to grab a shell-shaped paperweight, one of the few items on the desk, which included a laptop, desk phone, and an empty inbox tray.

"True ..." conceded Beanie.

However, he'd wanted to speak with Moreaux face-to-face. Beanie found that in-person interviews were more effective. Over the phone, a person could mask their tone. But, body language often revealed more than what a person said.

Upon arriving at Moreaux Investments and Insurance, a small office squeezed between a nail salon and a locksmith in a strip center near the airport, Beanie was shocked to learn that the company was a one-man operation, though Moreaux claimed he was looking for a secretary after he greeted Beanie with a gruff, "What do you want?"

Beanie wasted no time inquiring about an interview regarding Moreaux's recent arrest for the assault of Saul Biaggio. Following a few thunderous curses, Moreaux agreed to tell his side of the story, "to make sure people don't think I'm a knife-wielding fiend."

Clearing his throat, Beanie said, "So, speaking of knife-wielding fiends. Did you stab Saul Biaggio and leave him in the backyard to bleed to death?"

"No, but I wish I had," said Moreaux, letting loose a menacing chuckle. "Serves him right."

"You think he deserves to be in a medically induced coma?"

Scowling, Moreaux looked away. "I shouldn't have said that. It was terrible and I didn't mean it, but …"

"But?" prompted Beanie.

Moreaux shook his head and sighed. "Since my accident, things have not been right with me."

"What do you mean?" asked Beanie, though he suspected Moreaux was referring to the effects of the traumatic brain injury he'd suffered.

"I mean things are not right with my mind," said Moreaux. "With the way I think. I nearly cracked my head open in that accident. And it's had a negative effect on my mental state. I've suffered violent mood swings. Friends and family say I'm different. I've changed. And worst of all, I have blackouts …"

Frowning, Beanie asked, "Blackouts?"

"Sometimes, I don't remember things," said Moreaux. "Things I've said. Things I've done. I don't even know why I'm telling you this. What business is it of yours? And why would you care? But, sometimes I'll ramble. Or say whatever is in my head, no matter what it is, and …"

"And?"

Moreaux cleared his throat. "You said you had questions, right? Well ask them and get out. I have work to do. But I'm telling you right now, no comment."

Slightly jarred by the man's abrupt change of attitude, from contrite to belligerent, Beanie asked, "Can you tell me what happened the night of New Year's Eve? What did you do?"

"It's sort of fuzzy," began Moreaux. "I remember I didn't have plans.

I've been divorced for the last ten years and my kids live abroad. I think I was going to have a glass of Bishop's Reserve and go to bed."

"And is that what you think you did?" asked Beanie, eager to hear exactly what Moreaux remembered, considering the man's mental issues stemming from his accident.

"Like I said, it's fuzzy," said Moreaux. "But, I do remember talking to Saul."

"When?" Beanie asked. "Where were you?"

"I'm not sure, but … " Moreaux frowned. "I remember we argued."

"About what?"

"Probably the same thing we always argue about whenever we see each other," said Moreaux. "He's a heartless snake who stole the company we built together from me."

"Do you remember where the argument took place?"

Moreaux scratched his forehead. "I think we were outside."

"Outside," repeated Beanie, surmising that Moreaux might have forgotten the incident in the men's room at the Queen Palm during the Biaggio party.

"I remember the wind blowing," said Moreaux.

Beanie said, "Tammy Biaggio told the police that you ran her and Saul off the road, then you started beating against the window until Saul got out. Is that true?"

"Listen, I just said me and Saul argued," said Moreaux, scowling. "But I don't know anything about running him off the road and beating on the car window. Tammy probably made all that up. She doesn't like me because I sued Saul to get back what he stole from me."

Wary of getting the man riled up, Beanie said, "Let's go over the reasons why Detective Janvier arrested you—"

"That was a false arrest!" bellowed Moreaux. "And I told that two-bit detective as much and put him on notice that he will be hearing from my attorneys!"

"Well, Janvier does have compelling reasons to suspect you," said Beanie.

Scoffing, Moreaux said, "Goatwash!"

Taking a quick breath, Beanie said, "There's CCTV of you following Saul's Rolls in your black Mercedes."

"So the cops say," said Moreaux. "Videos can be faked. Tampered with."

"And CCTV of you at the gas station where the clerk says there was blood on your shirt."

Moreaux looked away. "I don't recall that."

"You went home, but then left twenty minutes later," said Beanie. "Your own camera surveillance shows that."

Frowning, Moreaux said nothing.

"Then you go to a seedy motel in Little Turkey—"

"That can't possibly be true," said Moreaux. "I wouldn't be caught dead in Little Turkey!"

"You left Little Turkey and went to your rental property in Oyster Farms," said Beanie.

Shaking his head, Moreaux said, "I don't recall."

Beanie said, "The cops found traces of Saul's blood in the backseat of your car."

"Not because I stabbed him and put him there," protested Moreaux, slamming the paperweight down as he leaned forward. "Somebody did but it wasn't me!"

"So, you think that same person used your knife to stab Saul?"

"That knife doesn't belong to me anymore," said Moreaux. "Saul gave it to me as a gift, but I gave it back to him after he stole the company out from under me. I didn't want it anymore."

"When did you give it back?" asked Beanie.

Moreaux opened his mouth, then closed it, shaking his head.

"You don't remember?"

"I know I gave it back because I didn't want anything from that vile spineless rat in my house," spat Moreaux. "Listen, I didn't stab Saul. I couldn't have, but ..."

"But?"

Moreaux's face fell, his expression apprehensive. "But, between me and you ... I don't know. The evidence is bad. And my mind. It doesn't work so good anymore. The doctors are trying to help, but ... "

Beanie said nothing, waiting for Moreaux to continue.

With a defeated sigh, the man slumped back in his chair, shaking his head. "What if the cops are right about me? What if I did stab Saul? What if I tried to kill him and I just don't remember."

The confession shocked Beanie and saddened him somewhat.

"But maybe you can help me."

"Help you … what?"

"Help me clear my name," said Moreaux. "You're a good investigative reporter. I read your stories. You know how to figure things out. Get to the truth."

Alarmed by the man's suggestion, Beanie sought to dissuade him. "Mr. Moreaux, I don't think—"

"You have to help me," beseeched Moreaux, abruptly leaning forward, his gaze wild and pleading. "Please. Maybe I stabbed Saul. Maybe I didn't. Either way, I have to know. If I did, then I need to pay for my crimes. But, if I didn't, I don't want to go to jail for a crime I didn't commit."

Beanie cleared his throat. "Mr. Moreaux—"

"I can't go to prison for something I didn't do," insisted Moreaux. "Please tell me you'll help me clear my name!"

23

"I really can't believe the police arrested Ken Moreaux." Ivan Rublev sighed and shook his head.

Sitting in one of the two chairs in front of Rublev's desk, Beanie scratched his chin.

Following his meeting with Kenneth Moreaux the day before, Beanie wasn't sure what to make of the disgruntled ex-business partner. One moment, Moreaux had been aggressive and combative. The next he was submissive and confused. Clearly, the man was suffering from mood swings due to the car accident. But what bothered Beanie most was Moreaux's startling admission that he might have blocked the memory of stabbing Saul.

The man's plea for help, which Beanie hadn't accepted, was also worrisome.

However, he hadn't refused to assist Moreaux in clearing his name.

At least, he wasn't going to refuse without talking to the employees at Biaggio Loans, Inc. first. Beanie wanted to get comments from them about Moreaux's arrest for another follow-up article. During the interview, he hoped to discern whether, or not, they thought Moreaux was capable of attacking Saul. Their answers would help Beanie determine if trying to help Moreaux clear his name was worth it, or a waste of time.

"Are you saying you don't think Moreaux could have stabbed Saul?"

"I'm not sure," said Rublev. "I suppose, when you think about it, in light of everything that's happened between Ken and Saul, it makes sense."

"What do you mean?"

"After Ken had the car accident, he started acting odd. Crazy mood swings. It was clear he'd suffered a mental breakdown. Saul didn't want to believe it, at first, but it was clear Ken had lost his mind. Eventually, Saul had to dissolve their business partnership."

Beanie scratched his chin. "And that's when Ken filed the lawsuit against him?"

"The lawsuits had no merit," said Rublev, leaning back in his chair. "All Ken did was nearly go bankrupt after all the legal fees he'd incurred. He's lucky Saul didn't counter-sue. I wanted him to."

"Why didn't he?"

"Saul would have been forced to disclose details about Ken's mental decline," said Rublev, eyebrows drawn together, expression concerned. "He didn't want to do that. Didn't want to tarnish Ken's reputation."

"It appears Saul was a good friend to Moreaux," said Beanie, recalling the story Umar, Noelle's cousin's boyfriend, had told him. Another instance of Saul protecting his former business partner.

"Which is why it will be a shame if Ken did stab Saul," said Rublev. "But, I suppose Ken's defense will be insanity."

Nodding, Beanie said, "Possibly."

"I'm afraid that I need to get back to work," said Rublev, standing. "With Saul still in the hospital, I'm shouldering more of the load than usual."

Recognizing that the controller was ending the interview, Beanie stood as well. "Of course. And thank you for talking to me."

"No problem," said Rublev. "Will you be talking to Lisette next?"

"I hope to," said Beanie. "If she's available."

Rublev gave him a tight smile, one that seemed to convey suppressed irritation. "Well, please remember that Lisette can become rather emotional when it comes to Ken Moreaux."

"Emotional?"

Rublev glanced away for a second, then said, "Lisette was very close to Ken Moreaux. And she was not happy about Saul's decision to remove Ken from the company."

"Well, that's understandable," said Beanie, staring at the controller. "Doesn't seem like it was an easy decision for Saul."

"What I mean is," said Rublev, picking up a file from his desk, and opening it. "You must take what Lisette says with a grain of salt."

Beanie frowned. "I'm not sure what—"

Rublev stared at him. "You must not believe everything that Lisette tells you …"

24

"I'm not sure I think that Mr. Moreaux stabbed Saul," said Lisette Javon, standing in front of a large whiteboard hanging on the wall opposite the door.

Sitting in the chair in front of the young woman's desk, Beanie tried to read what Lisette scribbled across the smooth, reflective surface but her small, chaotic writing was like a cross between chicken scratch and hieroglyphics.

After meeting with Ivan Rublev, Beanie traveled further down the corridor and around a corner to Lisette's office, a large space filled with natural light streaming through the wide picture window overlooking Pourciau Square. From the third floor, the quad teemed with tourists and residents, loitering and lounging, strolling purposely, and standing around. The day was bright and hot, with clusters of clouds floating across an azure sky, and a slight breeze shifting the palm fronds back and forth.

Beanie was still curious about the controller's warning about not believing Lisette, but he wasn't about to mention anything to the young woman. Besides, in Beanie's experience, those who called others liars were often liars themselves. He wondered if Rublev was worried that Lisette would say something that might cast suspicion on him.

"But the evidence against him is compelling," said Beanie.

Still facing the board, writing notes only she seemed to comprehend, Lisette said, "True, but …"

"But?"

"If Mr. Moreaux did anything wrong, it wasn't his fault," said Lisette. "He was having cognitive issues after the accident but I don't think …"

Beanie frowned. "You don't think … what?"

"Nothing."

"No, tell me please."

"I don't want to see my words in the newspaper," said Lisette, glancing over her shoulder to stare at Beanie. "I'll look disloyal."

"Disloyal?"

Lisette faced Beanie. "I really don't think I should say anything more."

Beanie didn't think the woman had said much of anything, so far, but to put her mind at ease, he said, "This conversation can be off the record if you like."

Sighing, Lisette said, "Concerning Mr. Moreaux, I don't think his mental issues would have crippled him forever. He'd talked to me about his plans to see a top neurologist at the Rakestraw-Blake Center."

"Really?" asked Beanie. Located in the neighboring Aerie Islands, the Rakestraw-Blake Center was a world-renowned medical center dedicated to the comprehensive care of neurological and psychological well-being. Beanie was quite certain the doctors there would be able to help Moreaux make a full recovery.

"I believed they would have helped him," said Lisette. "I told Saul as much, and he was happy about that. But then, he decided that Mr. Moreaux wasn't mentally fit to make business decisions. Saul and I disagreed on that. He allowed Ivan to persuade him to dissolve the partnership."

"Mr. Rublev told Saul he should get rid of Moreaux?"

Nodding, Lisette said, "Ivan was the first person to come to Saul complaining about Mr. Moreaux. Ivan told Saul that Mr. Moreaux's declining cognitive issues would lead to the downfall of the company.

He even told Saul that Mr. Moreaux was violent and unpredictable and might hurt him."

"But Mr. Moreaux suffered from violent mood swings," said Beanie. "He still does."

"I know that, but Saul didn't want to turn his back on his friendship with Mr. Moreaux," said Lisette. "He only did so, in my opinion, because he was listening to Ivan, which he shouldn't have done because …"

"Because …?" prompted Beanie, wishing the woman would stop trailing off.

Lisette's expression grew concerned. "I have no proof of this, so I would like to keep it between us but I don't think Ivan was sincere in his intentions when he persuaded Saul to get rid of Mr. Moreaux."

"Mr. Rublev wasn't sincere in his intentions?" Beanie frowned. "What do you mean?"

Biting her bottom lip, Lisette looked away, then said, "Well I think—"

The desk phone shrilled.

Frowning, Lisette looked at the phone. "I'm sorry, I have to take this."

"Thanks for your time," said Beanie as he stood, slipped out of the COO's office, and headed to the lobby.

The interviews with Ivan Rublev and Lisette Javon had been enlightening, interesting, and somewhat unexpected. There was Ivan Rublev's assessment of Moreaux as a sad man losing his mind. And Lisette's belief that Moreaux had been kicked out of the company unjustly, because of Rublev's influence over Saul. If that was true, maybe that was why Rublev had cautioned Beanie not to believe everything Lisette told him. The man might have suspected Lisette would mention his workplace shenanigans.

There was much to speculate, but Beanie would reserve his ruminations for a session with his coworkers, Stevie and Caleb. With the slacker and the curmudgeon, Beanie was sure he could come up with a theory about who was responsible for Saul Biaggio's current comatose state.

"You leaving?" asked the receptionist, giving him a sweet smile. "I thought you were talking to Lisette."

"She got a call," said Beanie. "But, I think our conversation was pretty much over."

"Did you ask them what they think about Mr. Moreaux being arrested?" asked the receptionist, her eyes dancing with mischievous delight. "I was shocked, but then I wasn't because I could totally see Mr. Moreaux stabbing Saul."

"Why is that?" asked Beanie.

"Don't get me wrong, I think Mr. Moreaux is a total sweetheart," began the receptionist. "But after his accident, he went *loco cabrito*, you know?"

Nodding, Beanie said, "The consensus seems to be that Mr. Moreaux suffered several cognitive malfunctions."

"Cognitive malfunction," said the receptionist. "Nice way to put it. The man lost his mind. The last time I saw him, he showed up unannounced, looking for Saul. I told him Saul wasn't here. He started screaming at me that I was lying. Then he drops a knife on my desk, and—"

"Wait. You said, a knife?"

Nodding, the receptionist said, "The knife Saul had given him. The hilt was engraved with Mr. Moreaux's name. It was a birthday present. Saul had me order it. Anyway, he drops the knife on my desk. Tells me it's evil and he doesn't want it because it's a cursed gift being used to control his mind."

"Interesting," said Beanie, although he actually thought it was sad. Physical sickness was terrible, but mental incapacity was terrifying. He couldn't imagine losing all sense of sound logic and reason.

"By that time, Lisette and Ivan come running out of their offices because I'm screaming, too, at this point," said the receptionist. "So, Ivan tells him to leave but Mr. Moreaux started cursing at him. And Lisette asked me what happened and I told her that Mr. Moreaux returned the knife Saul bought him, so she took it because we were scared Mr. Moreaux might get hold of it again, and then Ivan told me to call the police. So, I pick up the phone, and then Mr. Moreaux starts screaming that I'm not real."

Beanie frowned. "You're not real?"

"Yeah, had no idea what that meant," said the receptionist, rolling her eyes. "And he says Ivan is evil. He points at Lisette and says he knows the truth about her. Again, no idea what that meant. And then he says that Saul was planning to sacrifice us in a fire, or something—"

"Was Saul there?"

"No, he was on a business trip," said the receptionist. "Anyway, then the craziest thing happened."

"What?" asked Beanie, not sure he wanted to know.

"Mr. Moreaux just collapsed," she said. "We didn't know if he'd had a heart attack or a stroke or had fainted or dropped dead. I was calling an ambulance and Ivan was checking for a pulse when he came to. And he didn't know who we were. He didn't know where he was or how he'd gotten here. He didn't recall anything that had just happened."

25

"So, are you going to help Kenneth Moreaux clear his name?" asked Stevie, opening a bottle of water as he took a seat at the table where Beanie sat with Caleb.

An hour before noon might have been too close to lunch for a speculation session, but following his interviews with Ivan Rublev and Lisette Javon, Beanie needed a few different opinions from his own, which was that, inexplicably, Detective Janvier had arrested the right suspect—Kenneth Moreaux.

Beanie took a sip of his second cup of coffee of the day. "I don't think I can. All the evidence points to Moreaux as the person who stabbed Saul Biaggio."

"I don't know why you told that man you would help him," grumbled Caleb. "Waste of time and effort."

"Well, I actually didn't tell him that—"

"But you went to talk to the employees at Biaggio Loans to see what they thought," said Caleb, dropping sugar cubes into his coffee. "You must have thought they would tell you something that proved Janvier was wrong again. Hate to tell you, but this time Janvier might be right. Might as well just accept it and stop holding a grudge against the man."

Beanie nodded, stifling a chuckle as he wondered if the sugar would improve Caleb's mood. But he wasn't holding out much hope. The irascible old journalist had been a grump from the moment Beanie had met him, and he suspected—and expected—Caleb to remain cantankerous. What he didn't know was why Caleb was so sour. What had made the man a grump? What had caused the dour attitude? From what he knew, Caleb was a celebrated reporter, whose meticulous, investigative stories about The Fury had won him awards and worldwide acclaim. He was a family man, with a loving wife, several kids, and a grandkid, or two. Sure, his journalism skills had declined, and he was pretty much regulated to writing features and op-eds, but the man still lived a pretty good life. He had a nice home on a large piece of property on the outskirts of Adagio Bay, near the marina. He had his health. Didn't look his sixty-plus years.

Beanie suspected he would never know.

And he knew better than to ask Caleb.

"Maybe it's time for the means, motive, opportunity test," said Stevie. "Have you done it yet?"

"I didn't think I needed to," said Beanie. "Considering the evidence against Moreaux."

Stevie said, "But maybe there's something you overlooked that might call the arrest into question."

Caleb glared at Stevie. "And what in the unseasoned goat would Beanie have overlooked?"

"Stevie might be right," said Beanie. "Let's run through it. In terms of motive, Moreaux was livid that Saul kicked him out of the company."

"Which Biaggio only did because Moreaux was losing control of his mental faculties," said Caleb. "The man started having mood swings and blackouts."

"Even Moreaux fears that he might not remember stabbing Saul," said Beanie. "The aggressive behavior and blackouts have been witnessed by several people."

"I think that's what happened," concluded Caleb. "Moreaux lured Saul to that motel in Little Turkey. Stabbed him, then drove him to the rental house in Oyster Farms and left him in the backyard."

"But that's crazy," said Stevie. "Why would Moreaux dump Saul in the backyard of a house he owns? He's got to know the cops will be suspicious of him."

"That's what I can't wrap my head around," admitted Beanie.

Caleb scoffed. "I can't wrap my head around the two of you. You know why that seems crazy? Because Moreaux is crazy. If the man was in his right mind, he wouldn't have left Saul in his backyard. If the man was in his right mind, he wouldn't have stabbed Saul because he would still be able to make sound business decisions and he would not have been kicked out of the company."

"Well, yeah, right," said Beanie, taking a sip of coffee to combat the embarrassment of losing his own ability to reason and logically put things together.

Stevie cleared his throat. "Um, let's move on to opportunity."

"Moreaux has that, as well," said Beanie. "CCTV, camera surveillance, and the GPS in his Mercedes were all used to trace his movements that night. He leaves his home, goes to the seedy motel, calls Saul on a burner, Saul shows up at the same seedy motel, then he drives to the rental in Oyster Farms before driving back home."

Caleb said, "What about means?"

Beanie said, "The knife used to stab Saul was found in Moreaux's Mercedes when the police confiscated and searched it for evidence."

"I'll say he passes the suspect test," said Stevie, finishing his water. "Guess Janvier did get it right this time."

"But there is an issue about the knife," said Beanie. "Moreaux told me he gave it back to Saul. The receptionist at Biaggio Loans confirmed that."

Stevie frowned. "If Moreaux didn't have possession of the knife, how could he have stabbed Saul with it?"

"Exactly," said Beanie.

Even Caleb seemed stumped as he brought the cup of tea to his mouth for a sip.

"Anyway, one of the things I want to do is find out how Saul Biaggio's Rolls Royce ended up on a used car lot," said Beanie. "The CCTV and video surveillance shows Moreaux driving from Oyster Farms back to his house in Avalon Estates."

"I doubt Moreaux drove the Rolls from the motel," said Caleb.

Beanie said, "But, he could have. Suppose, after driving home, Moreaux called a cab and went back to the motel, where he got in the Rolls and drove it to the used car lot."

Stevie said, "It doesn't make sense, but it kind of does make sense because Moreaux is not in his right mind all the time."

Beanie said, "Right. So, if I can speak with the owner, I'd like to find out who sold him the Rolls."

An hour later, despite the lukewarm support from his coworkers, Beanie left the *Palmchat Gazette* and drove to Island Luxury Vehicles, a medium-sized lot crammed with a decent selection of expensive cars, most of them older models that had seen somewhat better days.

As Beanie walked through the maze of BMWs, Mercedes, and Volvos, a gusty wind whipped the palm trees surrounding the car lot, while a low deck of dark swirling clouds and the sharp, coppery scent in the humid air strongly indicated a burst of later afternoon thunderstorms.

He was several feet from the business office, which looked like an oversized shed made of stucco walls with a red-tiled roof, when the door opened and a short, weasel-like man hustled out to meet him.

Extending a hand and giving Beanie a bucked-tooth grin, the man introduced himself as Tony Reynolds. He was probably in his mid-forties, with caramel skin, a few lines around his eyes, and deeper grooves framing his mouth. Close-cropped salt-and-pepper curls clung to his head.

"Let me guess," said Reynolds. "You looking for a Corvette? Maybe a Ferrari?"

"No, actually—"

"You a family man?"

Nodding, Beanie said, "Yes, but—"

"A Volvo then," said Reynolds. "Safest car on the planet. How many kids you got? Three? Four?"

"Only two, but—"

"Volvo is perfect for a family of four," promised Reynolds. "Or, even an Audi. Safe, as well, but also fast so when you're alone without the wife and kids, you can go zero to sixty along the coast road in less than a minute.

Impressive, thought Beanie, but he said, "What I really need is—"

"A BMW," said Reynolds. "Ultimate driving machine."

"I'm Roland Bean from the *Palmchat Gazette*," Beanie rushed out while he could get a word in edgewise.

"*Palmchat Gazette*?" The man's smile faded as his eyes narrowed. "You a reporter?"

"Yes, and—"

"You might want to try Rocco's Rides over by the fish market near Rose Beach," said Reynolds, turning to walk away. "They have hatchbacks, small sedans, and—"

"I'm working on a story and wanted to ask the owner a few questions," said Beanie.

Tony Reynolds pivoted back to him, his smile returning. "Let's go into my office and talk."

Minutes later, seated in front of Reynolds' desk, Beanie surmised the man was willing to talk to him for one reason only: free publicity for his business. Unlike most witnesses, Reynolds had asked for reassurance that Beanie would spell his name, and more importantly the name of his business, correctly in the article.

"I won't take up too much of your time," began Beanie. "I wanted to ask about a Rolls Royce that—"

"Saul Biaggio's Rolls, right?" Reynolds leaned back and shook his head. "Man, if I had known that was his car, I never would have bought it."

"Have the police talked to you about it?" asked Beanie.

Shaking his head, Reynolds said, "Some cop called saying a detective might stop by but the guy never showed up so I figured they didn't care what I had to say."

"I'm surprised they didn't want to know who sold you the Rolls, considering it was stolen."

"I didn't know that at the time," insisted Reynolds, his gaze full of righteous indignation. "But I should have suspected, considering who sold me the car."

"Who was it?" asked Beanie. "Can you tell me?"

Shrugging, Reynolds said, "After he sold me a hot car, I'm not thinking about protecting him. It was a guy who was in Tiverton with my cousin. Two-bit car thief named Mick Guerra."

26

"Roland, what are you looking at?"

Snapped back to his wife's attention, Beanie stared at Noelle, frowning at him across the table they shared at Dizzy Jenny's, a popular, upscale beachfront restaurant. At eight o'clock at night, the place was crowded with a mix of tourists and local residents who enjoyed its excellent food, spectacular views of the orange and pink St. Killian, sunset, and romantic ambiance.

It was the perfect place for the monthly date night he and Noelle shared, just the two of them, without the rambunctious boys. The evening had been lovely, so far, and Beanie was about to suggest they indulge in one of the restaurant's decadent desserts when he turned his head to look for their waiter and instead saw—

"Roland?"

Beanie cleared his throat, then took a sip of water he'd drank to chase the cocktail he'd ordered. "Sorry. Just saw something I wasn't expecting to see."

Noelle frowned, leaning forward. "What?"

Sighing, Beanie said, "Remember earlier I told you about the used car salesman who bought Saul Biaggio's stolen Rolls Royce?"

Nodding, Noelle asked, "Is he here?"

"Not the salesman, no," said Beanie. "The guy who sold Reynolds the stolen car. Mick Guerra."

Her eyes widened, Noelle asked, "Are you serious?"

Beanie nodded. He'd immediately recognized the rangy man with the scruffy appearance at a table in the corner near the kitchen. After all, he'd spent the remainder of the workday researching Michael "Mick" Guerra, learning about his extensive rap sheet, and his stint in Tiverton, the maximum-security island prison. As Guerra was a car thief, Beanie figured the ex-con had been in the vicinity of the Little Turkey motel in the early hours of the new year, spotted the abandoned Rolls, and had stolen it.

A crime of convenience.

But considering the person Mick Guerra was dining with, Beanie was no longer sure of that assumption.

"And he's not alone," said Beanie.

"Who's he with?" asked Noelle. "Do you know?"

Confused and curious, Beanie said, "Ivan Rublev."

"Ivan Rublev?" Noelle shook her head. "The guy who works for Saul Biaggio? Why would he be talking to the man who stole Saul's Rolls Royce?"

"I'm not sure," said Beanie, discreetly glancing past his wife toward the table where Rublev and the scruffy car thief sat. The conversation looked intense, as the men leaned toward each other over the table.

"But, wait a minute," said Noelle. "There's really no proof that Mick Guerra stole the Rolls."

"If he didn't steal it, Elle, then how did he get it?" asked Beanie, still scoping the men. Rublev was now shaking his head and Mick Guerra stabbed his finger against the starched white tablecloth.

"Okay, well, I'm sure he obtained it illegally," said Noelle. "But, maybe he didn't steal it himself. Maybe he agreed to fence the car."

"Who knows?" asked Beanie. "The more important question is, what are Rublev and Guerra talking about?"

Noelle sighed, then took the last few sips of her white wine. "Any theories?"

"Nothing conclusive," said Beanie. "But the guy who may have stolen

Saul's Rolls talking to the guy who controls the books at Saul's business seems a bit shady."

At the table where the men sat, Guerra sat back, shaking his head while Rublev took a drink of what looked like rum.

Noelle asked, "You think Rublev told Guerra to steal Saul's Rolls? Or maybe knows that Guerra stole Saul's Rolls? But why? Or how?"

"If Rublev and Guerra are colluding about something, then what?" asked Beanie. "Maybe something that has nothing to do with Saul. But, I doubt it. And it makes me think of what Quincy Irving said about Rublev wanting to take over Saul's company."

"Quincy Irving accused Rublev of trying to kill Saul," said Noelle.

"And I thought Irving was deflecting at the time," said Beanie. "But what if there was some truth to his claim?"

Noelle said, "But all of the evidence points to Kenneth Moreaux."

Beanie scratched his chin. "Yeah, and maybe that's a bit too convenient. Maybe there's a reason Moreaux looks so guilty."

"You think—"

"One second …" interrupted Beanie, holding up a hand, his gaze on Guerra as the man jumped up, nearly knocking over the chair, and hurried out of the restaurant.

"What is it?"

"Guerra just left," said Beanie. "And he didn't look too happy."

"You should find out why," suggested Noelle.

Beanie pushed his chair back and stood. "I was thinking the same thing."

Moments later, standing near the chair Guerra had nearly knocked over, Beanie said, "Mr. Rublev, how are you?"

Rublev looked up and frowned. "I don't have time to talk right now."

"I don't want to talk," said Beanie, taking the seat Guerra vacated. "I just have a quick question. I saw you with Mick Guerra. I know he's the man who sold Saul's stolen Rolls Royce to a luxury car lot."

"He did what?"

"You didn't know?" asked Beanie, not sure if he should be skeptical, or not. Rublev looked genuinely shocked.

"I had no idea."

"Your conversation looked a bit intense," said Beanie.

Rublev exhaled. "That's putting it mildly."

"What do you mean?"

"I don't know anything about him stealing Saul's car," said Rublev. "What I know is he's an extortionist. He says he knows who stabbed Saul."

"Who was it?" asked Beanie, hardly able to believe he might have stumbled into a major scoop.

Shaking his head, Rublev said, "He refused to tell me. Said if I want to know who tried to kill Saul, I have to pay him for the information."

27

"No, thank you," said Beanie, politely declining the offer of a Palmito, the official cocktail of the Palmchat Islands, a delicious, refreshing blend of pineapple juice, rum, and mint leaves.

Standing at the outdoor bar, Florence Taylor shrugged, made a face, and then announced that Beanie didn't know what he was missing.

"Flo only uses Bishop's Reserve for her Palmitos," informed Chuck, Flo's husband, lying on a chaise lounge, enjoying his drink. "You should try one."

"Can't drink on the job," said Beanie, taking a seat on the divan across from the row of lounges on the expansive terrace that faced their back lawn, a mile of manicured emerald green grass accented by palm trees, lush tropical landscaping, and an Olympic-sized pool.

Thinking about the job, Beanie was anxious to get on with the business of his visit to the wealthy ex-pats, whose company he didn't always enjoy, though they were entertaining, and in the past had provided details that proved beneficial for Beanie's stories.

Apparently, Chuck Taylor had information regarding the Biaggio situation.

Beanie had received the call this morning while drinking his first cup of coffee and contemplating the conversation he'd had with Ivan

Rublev at Dizzy Jenny's during his date night with Noelle. Rublev's claim that Mick Guerra, the man who'd sold Saul's Rolls to the luxury used car lot, had tried to extort him for information about Saul's attack rang true. Beanie had immediately remembered his conversation with Rhea Calais, the nurse's aide.

When he walked in, Mrs. Biaggio didn't know who he was. He tells her he's someone who knows what happened to her husband. He tells her that if she wants to know who stabbed her husband, then she should call him.

Rhea had described the guy as scruffy. She'd told Janvier about him but the detective dismissed her claim as hearsay. Beanie couldn't help thinking the guy who'd approached Tammy Biaggio was Mick Guerra. He'd tried to get money from the worried wife but that hadn't worked so he decided to approach one of Saul's employees.

But did Mick Guerra really know who'd stabbed Saul? Or, was he a scammer trying to take advantage of a terrible situation? Hoping to profit off the pain of Saul Biaggio's family and friends. And if Guerra did know something, what information did he have? How did he know who had stabbed Saul? Had he witnessed the attack? Was he somehow acquainted with the attacker?

With those thoughts running amok in his head, Beanie had executed a quick public records search and discovered Mick Guerra's last known address. The ex-con was living in a rundown duplex near the airport. Beanie had knocked on the door, but no one answered. He'd been thinking Guerra might not reside at the location anymore when a neighbor walking by, holding a bag of trash, asked if he was "looking for Mick." Beanie replied in the affirmative, and the neighbor said Guerra wasn't home.

Beanie had been disappointed, but it was good to know he had the correct address.

Clearing his throat, Beanie stared at Chuck. Though shaded by the covering over the large terrace, the man was flushed and sweaty, like a parboiled lobster. "So, you have information about the Biaggio case?"

After another generous sip of his drink, Chuck said, "That we do."

"And we should have called you earlier, but on New Year's Day, we flew to our place in the Maldives," said Flo, pouring rum into a cocktail shaker. An amount that looked to Beanie like much more than the recipe required. "However, we've been faithfully following the story."

"It's riveting and fascinating," said Chuck.

"Sordid and sinister," agreed Flo, adding a hint of pineapple juice to her generous pour of rum.

"Thanks," said Beanie, wishing they'd get on with what they wanted to tell him. "And you have something to add to the story?"

Flo said, "Chuck and I went to the Biaggio's New Year's Eve party."

"Is that right?" asked Beanie, though he wasn't surprised. Chuck and Flo were active within the Avalon Estates social scene.

"It was a pretty good way to ring in the new year," said Flo, and then she made a face. "Not as elegant as I would have preferred, but nice. Not as tacky as it could have been."

Chuck nodded. "Nor as tawdry as we'd expected it might be."

Beanie chuckled slightly.

"Fortunately, Biaggio's wife hired an event planner," said Flo, walking to the lounge next to Chuck's. "If not, the place would have probably been decorated with hibiscus and seashells."

Not shocked by the horror on Flo's face or her blatant snobbery, Beanie said, "Did you see anything odd or strange or suspicious at the party?"

"Did we!" exclaimed Chuck. "That's why I had to call you."

Flo took a drink, then said, "Chuck saw Saul Biaggio arguing with the guy who does his books. What's his name? Young Russian guy. Igor Rabinov."

Confused, Beanie asked, "Arguing with his company controller? Ivan Rublev, you mean?"

Flo frowned. "Ivan Rublev?"

"That's his name. Ivan Rublev," said Beanie, holding in a chuckle as Flo gave him a skeptical side-eye. The woman was notorious for getting names wrong.

Chuck nodded. "Anyway, I saw Saul and Ivan arguing. Their voices were lowered but I could tell by their body language they were having a heated debate."

"Interesting," said Beanie.

"Chuck saw them in a small alcove near the men's room," said Flo.

"Naturally, I intervened," said Chuck. "Saul and Ivan claimed that everything was okay, but I could tell they were livid with each other."

Beanie stared at the sparks of sunlight glistening on the surface of the aquamarine pool water. "That is interesting. When I spoke with Ivan Rublev, he didn't mention an argument with Saul at the party."

Chuck scoffed. "Well, I suppose he wouldn't. Might give him a motive for stabbing Saul."

That it might, thought Beanie, returning to earlier ruminations of Quincy Irving's claims that Ivan Rublev had been angling to steal Saul's company to use it as a front for laundering Russian mob money. Maybe that idea wasn't so far-fetched, after all. And considering what Lisette Javon had told him about Ivan convincing Saul to kick Moreaux out of the company, the theory of Ivan Rublev as the mastermind behind Saul's stabbing might have some merit. "But, other than that, it was a great night," said Flo, her voice brimming with gossipy glee. "Oh, I have photos!"

Beanie started to protest. "I really don't—"

"I'll be back in two shakes of a goat's tail," she promised, wobbling slightly as she hurried toward the row of French doors leading into the house.

Minutes later, Flo sat next to him on the divan and angled her electronic tablet so he could see memories from the Biaggio New Year's Eve party.

"Here's me and Chuck and the Sampsons," said Flo, stopping at a photo of the couple with a couple who appeared to be a carbon copy of them. "Here's us with the Rideaux's."

Beanie recognized Harold Rideaux, the head of a power multi-million-dollar island construction firm. A few years back, he'd worked on a story involving the Rideaux family's alleged involvement in a bribery scheme.

"Oh, here's the one I wanted to show you," said Flo, handing him the tablet as she pointed to the group captured in a moment in time. "Me, Chuck, Saul and Tammy Biaggio, Ivan Rublev, and Lisette Javon. See how angry Ivan looks?"

"That was taken about twenty minutes after I saw Saul and Ivan arguing," said Chuck.

Beanie focused on the photo. At first glance, it was very wealthy people dressed expensively and having a good time at an elegant gala. But, upon closer inspection, he saw the tension in Saul's smile and the dourness in Rublev's flat expression.

"Ivan is definitely giving Saul the evil eye," said Flo, a bit too gleefully.

Beanie didn't think he would go that far, but Ivan didn't look pleased.

"And Lisette is wearing fake diamonds," said Flo, her voice dripping with disdain.

Focusing on the COO, Beanie stared at the diamond pendant hanging from her neck. He didn't know if it was a fake diamond, or not, but something about it—

"If you're not going to wear real diamonds," said Flo, "then don't wear them at all. So tacky."

Chuck said, "Flo and I really think the police should look into Ivan Rublev."

Flo finished her drink, then got up and slinked back to the bar. "He was obviously angry with Saul about something."

Chuck said, "Maybe angry enough to want to kill him."

28

"I don't know anything about Saul arguing with Ivan Rublev," declared Tammy Biaggio.

Beanie suppressed a sigh as he stared at Saul's wife, perched on the edge of a luxurious tufted divan like a queen on a throne, diamonds glittering around her neck, on her ears, on her wrist, and of course, on her ring finger.

After leaving the *Palmchat Gazette* with the intent of interviewing Tammy a second time, following his conversation with Chuck and Flo Taylor, Beanie suspected the conversation would devolve into a cat-and-mouse, tug-of-war for information.

When he'd arrived at the Biaggio mansion, which was constructed in the style of an Italian villa, the butler asked him to wait in the foyer, a spacious area that seemed larger than his kitchen. While he waited, Beanie figured he'd be told the lady of the house wasn't available, but to his surprise, moments later, she walked toward him, heels clicking on the marble tile.

After leading him into a sitting room, Tammy Biaggio requested refreshments from the butler and then invited Beanie to take a seat in the ornate room. They exchanged a few pointless pleasantries, and then Beanie inquired about her well-being.

Tammy Biaggio reported that she was doing as well as she could be, considering that her husband was still in the hospital, fighting for his life. She'd been visiting him every day, praying for him, and making sure he knew she was by his side. She'd been informed that patients often reported hearing their loved ones talking to them while they were comatose.

The butler brought tea, and Beanie declined a cup. As Tammy took dainty, polite sips, Beanie asked her about her husband's argument with Ivan Rublev at the New Year's Eve gala. Tammy had stared at him, her expression nonplussed, as though he'd picked up the teapot and sloshed hot liquid in her face.

Tammy denied knowing anything about an argument.

Beanie asked, "Are you aware of any contention between your husband and Ivan Rublev?"

Tammy placed the teacup on the saucer balanced on her knee. "Who told you that Saul argued with Ivan? Was it Kenneth Moreaux?"

Beanie said, "Actually, I can't—"

"You can't believe anything Kenneth tells you," said Tammy. "His mind is completely gone. He needs serious help. All Saul ever tried to do was help his friend. Moreaux had expressed interest in seeing doctors at the Rakestraw-Blake Center, and Saul was helping to facilitate that when Ken turned on him. He accused Saul of trying to sell his body to science so the doctors could probe his brain. That's why Ken stabbed Saul. He really thought Saul was out to get him. He is crazed and paranoid and he should be in jail for what he did to my husband."

"What if Kenneth Moreaux didn't stab Saul?"

Tammy pursed her lips. "You know better than me that the evidence against Ken is solid. It was detailed in your article. If Ken didn't stab Saul, then who did?"

"Ivan Rublev, maybe?" suggested Beanie. "I have a trusted source who says Saul and Ivan Rublev had a very heated argument at the New Year's Eve party."

Tsking her annoyance, Tammy shook her head. "Saul didn't say anything to me about an argument with Ivan. And if that's true, then they probably argued about Ken."

"Why would they argue about him?"

Her heavily lined eyes narrowed, Tammy said, "I'm not saying they did. But, Ivan didn't agree with Saul's plans to help Ken. Ivan was worried about Saul. Afraid that Ken might hurt Saul, and as you know, Ivan was right."

"I'd like to ask you about Quincy Irving," said Beanie.

Tammy made a sour face. "The man who tried to kill my husband while he was in ICU? The man who might get away with it because the prosecutors are questioning the nurse's story? Quincy obviously wanted to kill Saul for firing him."

Beanie said, "Quincy Irving believed Ivan Rublev was working for the Russian mob. Could there be any truth to that? Because I found out from a source that Irving owed money for gambling debts to the PC-5. But this source, who would know, said there was no indication that Irving was laundering money for the mob."

"Listen, I don't know anything about money laundering or the mob or any of that," snapped Tammy. "What I know is that Kenneth Moreaux stabbed my husband! That's what you should be focusing on."

Beanie said, "Mrs. Biaggio, I'm just trying to make sure an innocent man isn't put in jail for something he didn't do."

"Innocent man?" Tammy scoffed. "You really think Ken is innocent? Well, let me show you something. I'll be right back."

Minutes later, Tammy Biaggio returned with a smartphone.

Thrusting it toward him, she said, "I want you to take a look at this video."

"What is this?" asked Beanie, intrigued.

"What I was going to show you at the hospital," said Tammy. "You probably don't remember but we were talking and I was about to tell you about this video I recorded but then the nurse came to get me because the doctor had information about Saul's condition."

Vaguely recalling the incident, Beanie took the phone.

The screen was paused on what appeared to be a chaotic scene. He pressed the 'play' button. Immediately, he saw the chaos. In the video, shot at night, from a position possibly several feet away, Kenneth Moreaux swung his fists toward Saul Biaggio, who was clearly trying to defend himself. Moreaux landed several punches to the side of Saul's head before Saul struck back, hitting Moreaux in the nose. Blood dripped down Moreaux's face, but he kept coming for Saul, screaming and cursing as Saul repeatedly told him to calm down. Tammy's voice could be heard in the background, shouting for the men to stop fighting. However, Moreaux continued threatening to kill Saul.

Pointing a wobbly finger at Saul, he sneered, "You won't live to see the new year, you wicked snake!"

Saul looked into the camera, and said, "Stop filming! Now! Put the phone away!"

The video ended with Tammy's voice. "I'm calling the police!"

Tammy said, "But I didn't. That was the worst mistake I ever made. If I had, Saul wouldn't be fighting for his life right now."

"Saul didn't want you to call the police?" surmised Beanie, still disturbed by what he'd seen.

Shaking her head, Tammy said, "Saul wanted to protect Ken. He didn't want Ken to go to jail. He actually told me to delete the video, but I'm glad I didn't. And now I have a question for you. Do you still think Kenneth Moreaux is so innocent?"

29

"That video Tammy Biaggio showed you sort of puts the final nail in Moreaux's coffin," said Stevie.

Caleb nodded. "I agree. Moreaux did it. But, I always thought that. Just look at the evidence."

"The evidence," said Beanie, taking a sip of what would probably be his last cup of coffee of the day.

After his interview with Tammy Biaggio, he'd returned to the *Palmchat Gazette* and corralled his coworkers into the breakroom to share the latest developments.

"Crazy to think that Janvier got it right this time," said Stevie.

"Sad situation, though," said Caleb, shaking his head. "Moreaux probably doesn't even remember stabbing Saul."

Beanie said, "Because maybe he didn't."

Exhaling, Caleb asked, "Why can't you just admit that Moreaux did it? Is it because you don't want Janvier to be right because you can't stand the man?"

Shaking his head, Beanie said, "No, it's because of the knife. The more I think about it, the more I don't believe that Moreaux passes the "means" test. I keep asking myself, how did Moreaux get the knife that was used to stab Saul? Yes, Saul gave the knife to Moreaux as a present.

But, Moreaux gave it back. The receptionist at Biaggio Loans confirmed that. So how did Moreaux get the knife back and use it to stab Saul?"

Stevie picked up his water bottle and took a sip.

Caleb sighed. "Okay, you're right about that. The knife is the one thing that doesn't add up. There's no explanation of how Moreaux got the knife."

"And until there is an explanation," said Beanie. "I'm not going to be convinced that Moreaux stabbed Saul."

Ten minutes later, back at his desk, Beanie grabbed a notepad and a pen. On the paper, he wrote, How can Moreaux pass means test? Then, he set about to answer his question. Half an hour later, all he had to show for his efforts were implausible, illogical situations that strained credibility.

He considered that the knife might have been in the Rolls Royce. Or, perhaps, when Saul left his house to meet Moreaux at the seedy motel, he'd bought the knife with him for protection. During a fight, Moreaux took the knife from Saul and stabbed him with it.

Another scenario had Moreaux demanding the knife be returned to him. As the man's mind was addled, he might have forgotten that he'd given the knife back, and then decided he wanted to keep it.

Beanie had considered the possibility that Moreaux had lied about returning the knife and then bribed the receptionist to corroborate his story.

He wondered if the police might have been wrong about the murder weapon. Perhaps, they mistakenly identified the knife.

Exhaling, Beanie leaned back, staring at his handwritten ruminations.

None of his speculations made any sense. He tore the page from the pad, then balled it up, and—

His desk phone rang.

Tossing the paper into the waste basket, he answered. "Roland Bean."

"Mr. Bean, this is Ivan Rublev."

Curious, Beanie asked, "How can I help you?"

"I won't beat around the bush," said Rublev. "I believe I know who tried to kill Saul Biaggio."

"Shouldn't you be calling the police?"

On the other end of the line, Rublev sighed. "I have spoken with Detective Janvier but he's convinced it was Kenneth Moreaux and is not interested in my amateur sleuth theories, as he called them."

"Sounds like Janvier," said Beanie.

"You remember the man you saw me with at Dizzy Jenny's?" asked Rublev.

"Mick Guerra?"

"Right," said Rublev. "He's the man who stabbed Saul. It wasn't Moreaux."

"How do you know it was Guerra?" asked Beanie.

"Can you meet me at the Biaggio offices tonight? Say around eight p.m.?"

Wary, Beanie asked, "Why so late?"

"I need time to get the evidence together," said Rublev. "But when I show it to you, you'll see that I'm right."

"Mr. Rublev, before you go," said Beanie, recalling his conversation with Chuck and Flo Taylor. "When we speak tonight, there's something else I'd like to ask you."

"What is that?" asked Rublev.

"A source of mine claims to have seen you arguing with Saul Biaggio at the New Year's Eve party," said Beanie. "I'd like to know what that was about."

"That was about nothing," snapped Rublev. "Kenneth Moreaux had a meltdown in the bathroom and Saul didn't want to call the cops and have him thrown out. We disagreed about that. But, there's no need to discuss that. The point of our meeting needs to be the evidence against Guerra."

30

The sun had already set by the time Beanie headed across Pourciau Square toward the three-level orange building where the office of Biaggio Loans, Inc. was located.

Below the orange and purple-streaked sky, hundreds of tourists and island residents mingled, enjoying the festive atmosphere of food trucks and live music. As Beanie entered the orange building, the sounds of laughter, conversation, and calypso music faded, overtaken by the hushed hum of machinery, A/C units, and other mechanical and electrical components that created most of the sound when an office building was empty.

On the elevator, the absence of occupants was like a dull roar that only increased when the doors opened and he was confronted with a dimly lit hallway. To conserve energy, the majority of the overhead recessed lights were off. Every fourth light was on, but it created dark shadows that shrouded the hall. Stretching before him, the corridor made him feel a bit wary, as though something might be lurking in the gloom.

Beanie wasn't a superstitious or easily spooked person, but he felt goosebumps as he continued down the hallway, now and again looking over his shoulder, as he advanced toward Biaggio Loans.

Behind the frosted glass door, the lights were dimmed. Beanie could make out an overhead light above the receptionist's desk. The place looked deserted, which was strange considering Rublev had requested to meet him. With an exhale, Beanie grabbed the handle and opened the door. Inside, the sitting area was darkened but Beanie could discern furniture and shapes enough to make his way to the receptionist's desk.

"Mr. Rublev," Beanie called out, wondering, once again, why he'd agreed to meet the man.

Beanie wasn't even certain he believed the controller. On his drive to Pourciau Square, he'd reflected on the man's surprise call. Out of the blue, Rublev declares he knows that Mick Guerra—the man who may or may not have stolen Saul's Rolls but definitely sold it to a used car dealer—stabbed Saul. But, he couldn't give Beanie the reasons for his allegations. In hindsight, Beanie figured he should have been more suspicious.

He no longer knew what to think about Ivan Rublev, but he wasn't sure he trusted the man. Maybe Quincy Irving had been right about him? Maybe Rublev, in an effort to use Saul's business to launder money for the mob, had orchestrated Saul's stabbing.

Looking toward the interior hallway, Beanie spotted the lone light in the dark corridor.

It spilled from Rublev's office.

The man was here. Why hadn't he answered Beanie?

As he headed down the hallway, Beanie wondered if Rublev had hired Mick Guerra to stab Saul and was now betraying the man. Rublev claimed the conversation at Dizzy Jenny's had been Guerra's attempt to extort him for information. The truth might have been that Guerra wanted more money for stabbing Saul. Rublev might have refused because Guerra hadn't killed Saul, which could have been what Rublev wanted.

Coming abreast of the door to Rublev's office, Beanie knocked on the frame before stepping inside.

"Mr. Rublev … "

Beanie stopped, his heart slamming.

Ivan Rublev was slumped in his chair, dead from a gunshot wound between his eyes.

31

"As of right now," said Fields, his jovial voice ringing out from the speaker phone on Beanie's desk in his tiny cubical at the *Palmchat Gazette*. "Janvier doesn't have any suspects."

Two days had passed following Beanie's gruesome discovery of Ivan Rublev's dead body. The gunshot wound in the center of the man's forehead had remained with Beanie, causing him to toss and turn. His article, BIAGGIO LOANS EXECUTIVE SHOT DEAD had done well, with lots of engagement, likes, shares, and hundreds of comments.

Beanie struggled to process the fact that had he arrived earlier, he might have been able to prevent the murder or might have seen the murderer, or could have been killed himself.

Pushing aside the sobering thoughts, Beanie asked, "What about Mick Guerra? When Janvier questioned me, I told him that Rublev suspected Guerra had stabbed Saul."

Fields said, "You know Janvier. It's all hearsay unless you have proof."

Beanie sighed his frustration. "But, still, I would think he'd question the man. Considering that I also told him about the meeting between Rublev and Guerra at Dizzy Jenny's."

Nodding, Fields said, "If it was up to me, Guerra would be my main suspect. He should be questioned about the extortion attempt. I'd also want to know why Rublev would suspect him of stabbing Saul."

Exhaling, Beanie said, "Just wish I knew what evidence Rublev wanted to show me."

"He didn't give you any idea of what it might be about?"

Beanie shook his head. "But, I've been thinking it might have something to do with money laundering. I remember Rublev telling me he believed that Quincy Irving was using the company to launder money."

"Which is why Saul fired Irving," said Fields. "He believed Irving was washing cash for the Russian mob."

"Rublev was trying to prove it," said Beanie. "He told me he'd traced the dirty money to secret numbered accounts at a bank in the Caymans. A friend there was going to help him find out who the secret accounts belonged to."

Fields said, "Maybe that's the evidence Rublev wanted to show you?"

"And maybe the evidence pointed to Guerra?"

Fields said, "But Rublev told you that Guerra stabbed Saul, right? So, wouldn't the evidence he wanted to show you have something to do with that?"

Beanie said, "Maybe Rublev found out that Guerra had something to do with the money laundering."

"But how?" asked Fields. "Guerra didn't work at Biaggio Loans. Unless he was working with someone at the company."

Beanie nodded. "Maybe Quincy Irving."

"You think it's been him all this time?"

Beanie didn't know.

But he knew someone who would ...

Two hours later, after a quick lunch at his favorite food truck in Pourciau Square, Beanie drove to the Purple Gecko for an impromptu meeting with Lime Shoes. The old gangster wasn't exactly happy that Beanie hadn't called before he'd stopped by, but he was willing to talk.

"Didn't we already have this conversation?" grumbled Lime Shoes when Beanie asked him about Quincy Irving possibly working for the Russian mob.

"I just want to make sure there's no possibility that Quincy Irving was using Saul's company to launder money," said Beanie.

Lime Shoes fingered his shark's tooth necklace. "I'll be honest with you. The Russians aren't a big deal. They don't cause problems. They pay their taxes. So, I don't hear much about them because I'm not really listening, you understand? I'm not interested. Was Quincy Irving making their cash clean? I don't know. Maybe. Maybe not."

"That's actually good to know," said Beanie, reflecting on his theory about Quincy Irving and Mick Guerra working together. Considering Irving's gambling debts, Beanie could see the man agreeing to work for the Russian mob. The money he received could help him pay off the PC-5. However, when Saul fired him, Irving might have hired Mick Guerra to kill Saul. Irving probably thought that Tammy—who had no ill will toward Irving and didn't really believe Rublev's claims that Irving was laundering money—would agree to let him run her deceased husband's company. At that point, Irving would continue his association with the Russian criminals.

But things hadn't turned out like that.

Instead, Saul ended up in the hospital, instead of dead. So, Irving tried to finish him off, but he'd been caught by a nurse. With no income, Irving most likely couldn't pay Guerra his fee for attacking Saul. So, Guerra went first to Tammy, hoping to secure funds for information about Saul's killer. When that didn't work, Guerra went to Rublev.

Somehow, Guerra must have found out that Rublev figured out his part in Saul's stabbing, so Guerra killed Rublev.

"Speaking of things that are good to know," said Lime Shoes.

Sensing an ominous change in the old gangster's mood, Beanie swallowed. "What's that?"

Lime Shoes finished his drink and sat the glass down on the table, forcibly enough to make Beanie jump slightly. "Why is that cop really interested in my daughter?"

32

Ethan swung the cricket bat and whacked the red ball across the back lawn, nearly all the way to the opposite fence.

Beanie had set up a wicket, constructed from wooded stumps and bails, at the far opposite end of the backyard, as far away from the shed as possible. But as he glanced toward the structure, where the ball had traveled, his mind transported him back to New Year's Eve, when Saul Biaggio had, somehow, found his way over the fence and into the backyard, bleeding from stab wounds to his chest.

"Did you see, Daddy!" Shouted Ethan, full of excitement and triumphant pride. "Told you I was getting better! I've been practicing!"

"I see that," said Beanie, giving his son an exploding fist bump when the rambunctious rascal ran up to him, smiling, his eyes alight with buoyant glee.

"Good job!" said Noelle, who held Evan in her arms.

"Good job!" Evan echoed, laughing, and clapping his hands. "Good job!"

"I'm going to find the ball, Daddy," announced Ethan, running toward the fence.

"Find the ball!" said Evan, squirming in Noelle's arms. "Put me down, Mommy! Find the ball!"

Not surprised that little Evan wanted to go running off after his big brother, Beanie squeezed the little monster's nose before Noelle lowered him to the ground. Immediately, he took off as fast as his chubby legs could carry him.

"And when Lime Shoes asked you about Fields' intentions with Amber, what did you say?"

Catching the irritation in his wife's tone, Beanie turned to her. The smile she'd bestowed upon her sons was gone. In its place was a scowl and pursed lips.

Beanie sighed.

Following his visit to Lime Shoes, Beanie had returned to the *Palmchat Gazette* to finish up a few assignments, including starting another follow-up draft about the Biaggio case. He planned to focus on potential suspects, but needed input from Vivian, and possibly the legal department, about what should and should not be included in the article. His boss, however, had left work early, so he put the task on his to-do list for the following day.

With his day done, he'd picked up the boys from their grandmother's house in Handweg, then headed home. After a light snack, he and the kids decided to set up a makeshift mini cricket field in the backyard. Ethan played cricket at school and had been asking to join the neighborhood little league team, which he would have to try out for. For preparation, Ethan had requested a practice field. Beanie had finally gotten around to obliging his son.

Beanie, Ethan, and Evan had been in the backyard doing drills when Noelle came home. Between batting practice, Beanie had given his wife snippets and snatches of the meeting with Lime Shoes.

"I told Lime Shoes that Fields likes Amber," answered Beanie, keeping his eye on the boys, who seemed to have abandoned their search for the cricket ball in favor of chasing a lizard.

"And what did he say?" asked Noelle, crossing her arms.

Beanie reflected on the conversation, remembering Lime Shoes' response. "And what exactly does he like about her?"

"Amber is a wonderful woman," Beanie had said, desperate to de-escalate the situation before it got out of control, which he had a feeling it might, considering the scowl on Lime Shoes' face. "As I'm sure you know. She's kind and sweet and—"

"And she has a father in the PC-5," interrupted the old gangster.

"I don't think Fields is concerned about that," said Beanie.

"Oh, you don't?" challenged Lime Shoes. "He's an officer of the law. And I break the law. And you think he's not concerned about that?"

"What I meant was," said Beanie, not quite sure how to explain what he meant. "I don't think … that is, Fields doesn't … well, you see—"

"While you're trying to figure out what it is you want to say," said Lime Shoes, "I'll say this. I have always been straight with you. When you come to me with questions, I answer you, or I don't. I don't hem and haw with you, so don't hem and haw with me."

Feeling as though he'd been rapped on the knuckles by a reprimanding headmaster, Beanie sat up straight.

"Now tell me this," said Lime Shoes. "Is this cop planning to use my daughter to get to me?"

Not surprised by the question, Beanie shook his head. "That is not Fields' intention. As a matter of fact, he doesn't want to have anything to do with you. I mean, he wants his relationship with Amber to be separate from your relationship with her."

"Well, that's not what Amber wants," said Lime Shoes, his tone perturbed. "She wants us to meet. Have dinner. Get to know each other."

"How do you feel about that?" asked Beanie, though he had an idea.

Lime Shoes sneered at him. "How do you think I feel? I don't want to break bread with a cop. Especially not a cop who I suspect is only going out with my daughter so he can trick her into getting evidence against me which he will use to try to put me in Tiverton."

Noelle shook her head. "And were you able to convince him that Fields is not trying to use Amber? That he really likes her? He wants a future with Amber. Maybe marriage. Kids. He could care less who her father is."

Beanie scratched the back of his neck as a warm, salty breeze rushed across his face. "I think I was able to do that, but …"

"But?"

Exhaling, Beanie said, "But I don't really know …"

Noelle frowned. "You don't know what?"

"I don't know that Fields is not planning to go after Lime Shoes," admitted Beanie. "I don't know that he won't ask Amber for information against her dad."

"Roland, are you serious?" Noelle pinched the bridge of her nose. "You know how Fields feels about Amber. You know he's not going to jeopardize the relationship to collar some crook who will most likely beat the charges."

Beanie rubbed his eyes. "Yeah, but I'm also worried that Fields might be pressured to get evidence against Lime Shoes. He's keeping the relationship with Amber lowkey, for now. He doesn't want his superiors to know he's seeing the daughter of a PC-5 member."

"You think Fields' bosses would force him to go undercover?"

"I don't know," said Beanie. "But that's what concerns me."

"Daddy! Daddy!" shouted Ethan and Evan. "We got the ball!"

Beanie clapped and beckoned his kids toward him. "Great! Come on back so I can bowl you a few more balls."

Dropping the subject of Lime Shoes, Fields, and Amber, Noelle encouraged the boys to continue the game. Beanie was thankful they were tabling the subject, for now. He wanted to focus on having fun with his kids. Later, he would ruminate on an additional worry …

The idea of Lime Shoes forcing Fields to become a PC-5 mole.

33

As the elevators closed, Beanie took a deep breath.

Once again, he was in the orange-painted multi-level building where Biaggio Loans, Inc. housed its offices on the third floor. Twenty minutes ago, walking from the *Palmchat Gazette* to Pourciau Square, Beanie had taken advantage of the perfect afternoon weather to interview the remaining employees at Biaggio Loans, Inc. for a quick follow-up article. Since Detective Janvier had yet to name a potential suspect in the murder of Ivan Rublev, Beanie hoped to ask Lisette Javon and the receptionist if they had any ideas on who might have killed Ivan Rublev.

Beanie's money was on Mick Guerra.

Not only had Guerra tried to extort Rublev, but Rublev himself had claimed to have proof that Guerra had stabbed Saul. When he arrived at work that morning, while making his first cup of coffee of the day, Beanie remembered Guerra's involvement with Saul's stolen Rolls Royce.

However, that detail was still hard to reconcile.

Initially, considering the damaging evidence against Kenneth Moreaux, it appeared that Moreaux had lured Saul to the seedy Little Turkey motel, then stabbed Saul, and put him in the backseat of the Mercedes. Finally, Moreaux drove the Mercedes to his rental home in

Oystery Farms and dumped Saul in the backyard, most likely thinking the man was dead.

But, if Guerra had stabbed Saul, then did that mean Guerra had put Saul in the Mercedes and drove the man to Moreaux's rental home? But, no, that didn't make sense. CCTV and other video surveillance showed Moreaux returning home in his black Mercedes.

Beanie couldn't figure out how to make it make sense.

Unless Mick Guerra was working with Kenneth Moreaux.

Could Moreaux have hired Guerra to help him attack Saul? Was it possible that Moreaux lured Saul to the motel, where Guerra was waiting to ambush him? Then after Guerra stabbed Saul, Moreaux put Saul in the backseat of his Mercedes and drove him to Oyster Farms. In the meantime, Guerra took Saul's Rolls Royce and sold it to the used car dealer.

A diabolical plot, definitely, but Beanie thought it might have played out that way.

And, if so, he might have to consider Kenneth Moreaux as a potential suspect in the murder of Ivan Rublev, as well.

The elevators opened.

Approaching the double, wood-framed glass doors of Biaggio Loans, Inc., Beanie opened one of the doors and entered the office foyer.

The receptionist greeted him with a nod of recognition.

"How are you, Mr. Bean?" she asked.

"Please call me Beanie," he said, suddenly feeling much older than his thirty years. "Mr. Bean is my dad."

"Okay, then, Beanie it is," she said. "What can I do for you? As I'm sure you can imagine, Lisette and I are trying to process what happened to Ivan. It's been very difficult. The police just allowed us to return to the office today. They've been here collecting evidence since you found Ivan."

"I'm guessing the police questioned you and Ms. Javon?"

Nodding, the receptionist said, "We both had to go down to the station. A routine interview. You know, do you know who might have wanted Ivan dead? Questions like that."

Beanie asked, "Do you know who wanted Ivan dead?"

Eyes widened, the receptionist shook her head. "It's so crazy! First Saul got stabbed. Then Ivan gets killed. I'm like, what is going on at this place? Are Lisette and I next? Maybe I should quit? I feel like I'm living in a true crime podcast, you know? My roommates and I had been trying to figure out who stabbed Saul and now we have to guess who could have murdered Ivan Rublev. And, like I told you, I have no clue."

"Do you recall Mr. Rublev mentioning a man named Mick Guerra?" asked Beanie, propping an elbow on the crescent-shaped console.

Her eyes dancing with mischievous glee, the receptionist said, "Mick Guerra? No. Why? Is he a suspect? Did he kill Ivan?"

"Mr. Rublev was suspicious of him," Beanie said. "He told me that he thought a man named Mick Guerra had stabbed Saul."

"Are you serious?" The receptionist gasped. "Why would this Mick Guerra want to kill Saul?"

"That's what Mr. Rublev was going to tell me," said Beanie. "I found his body because I was going to meet him to talk about some evidence he wanted to show me. Evidence connecting Mick Guerra to the attack on Saul."

"That's so crazy," said the receptionist. "Wait until I tell my roommates. Katie, she's one of my roommates, was questioning Mr. Moreaux as the killer because she couldn't figure out how he got the knife back when he gave it back to Saul."

"Yeah, I was wondering that, as well," admitted Beanie.

"And the only thing I could come up with was that Mr. Moreaux stole the knife from Lisette, because other than that—"

"Wait a minute." Beanie stopped her. "What did you say? About stealing the knife from Lisette? I thought you said Moreaux gave the knife back to you and then you gave it to Saul?"

Shaking her head, the receptionist said, "No, remember, Mr. Moreaux dropped it on my desk. Then he started screaming and cursing. That's when Ivan and Lisette came out of their offices."

"Right," said Beanie, trying to recall the version of events she'd told him.

"And then, once we got Mr. Moreaux calmed down," said the

receptionist, "Lisette took the knife and said she'd give it back to Saul, which was fine by me because—"

"Mr. Bean, I wasn't expecting you today."

Recognizing Lisette's soft tone, Beanie turned from the receptionist, who'd made a quick, sheepish face before hurrying to sit and busy herself with a stack of documents.

"I'm sorry," said Beanie. "I should have called first but I was in the area and thought I'd stop by."

"For what?" asked Lisette, folding her arms across her chest. "We don't have time to be interviewed. With Ivan's passing and Saul still in a coma and Quincy Irving gone, the company is free-falling into turmoil and I can't allow that to happen. Saul has been too good to me, and—"

"I understand," said Beanie, spotting something odd on her left hand. A gauze bandage wrapped around it.

"We have no idea who wanted to kill Ivan," said Lisette, walking into the foyer, toward the door. "That's the only statement we care to make at the time."

Recognizing that he was being dismissed, Beanie met Lisette at the door, which she held open for him.

"Before I go," he started. "I wanted to ask you if you ever heard Mr. Rublev mention a man named Mick Guerra?"

Lisette frowned, then shook her head. Her voice lowered, she whispered, "Mr. Bean, all I can say, is that I hope no one else at this company is targeted because of some scheme Ivan Rublev was involved in."

"A scheme?"

Continuing to whisper, her expression anxious, Lisette said, "I've been going through Ivan's files and ..."

"And?"

Shaking her head, Lisette said, "Things are not adding up. That's all I can say. I must get back to work. Have a good day."

34

An hour later, back at the *Palmchat Gazette*, Beanie turned to his computer and accessed the public records database employed by the *Palmchat Gazette* staff.

His conversations with the receptionist and Lisette Javon had yielded nothing. He'd been hoping one of them would have additional information about Mick Guerra, the man Ivan Rublev suspected of stabbing Saul Biaggio, but he'd had no luck.

He figured he needed to talk to Guerra himself, but when he returned to the man's last known address, the door had, once again, gone unanswered. Beanie left frustrated, deducing that Guerra was no longer staying at the dilapidated duplex.

After a quick conversation with Caleb in the breakroom, Beanie planned to look up the parole officer of Mick Guerra. He clicked on a link to the Palmchat Island Parole Records search and entered Guerra's name. Moments later, he wrote down the parole officer's contact information and gave the man a call.

"Funny you should call," said the officer, after Beanie introduced himself and stated his business.

"Why is that?" asked Beanie.

"I'm looking for Guerra myself," the parole officer said. "He's not living at his current listed address."

"So you have no idea where he is or how to get in touch with him?" asked Beanie.

"Didn't say that," the man chuckled. "Got some information from a guy who knows him and claims he's living in some motel in Little Turkey."

"A motel in Little Turkey?" Beanie echoed, thinking of the motel Kenneth Moreaux had lured Saul Biaggio to. Could it be the same motel? If so, it would give credence to Beanie's theory that Guerra might have been working with Moreaux to ambush Saul.

"The guy didn't give me a name," said the parole officer. "And I don't have time to visit every motel in that neighborhood."

Beanie said, "I think I might know the motel Guerra might be staying at. If I find him there, I'll give you a call."

An hour or so later, Beanie turned his SUV into the small parking lot of the Seahorse Inn. The vehicle jostled as the cracked concrete presented a challenge to his car's suspension. Steering his wheel left, then right, to avoid a large pothole, which looked more like a crater, Beanie found a space near the motel's office.

Outside, the heat broiled while the wind, though blustery, did little to provide a respite.

Inside, unfortunately, was no better.

The office was small, stuffy, and slightly damp, serviced by a rickety ceiling fan that clicked with each revolution.

Sitting behind a scarred wooden desk in the corner was a West Indian man of medium height and indeterminate age with a rotund belly beneath a T-shirt straining to contain his girth. With a smile and a hearty greeting of hello, the man grunted as he struggled to his feet.

"Need a room?"

Beanie shook his head and returned a quick smile. "Actually, my name is Roland Bean. I'm a reporter at the *Palmchat Gazette*."

"Roland Bean," said the man, extending a plump hand as he approached the counter. "I seen your name in the paper. I don't read it much, but my wife does. Good to meet you. I'll have to tell Elenore I met you."

"Thank you," said Beanie, shaking the man's hand. "Listen, I don't want to take up too much of your time—"

"It's okay. You're the first person who's walked in all day," said the motel clerk. "Slow day. You working on a story?"

Nodding, Beanie said, "I'm looking for a witness I've been trying to interview. I know you can't reveal the identity of anyone who's staying at your motel—"

"It's fine. This ain't the Queen Palm," said the motel clerk. "They don't pay enough for anonymity. Who're you looking for?"

Shocked by the man's blatant disregard for his occupants' privacy, Beanie cleared his throat. "A man named Mick Guerra."

The clerk tilted his head left and right, then looked up at the ceiling. "Hmmm ... the name does not ring a bell, but I never really pay attention to names. My establishment is cash only. I don't even require I.D. Like I said, I know this place isn't the Queen Palm. People don't come here to see and be seen. They come to hide."

"I see," said Beanie, kicking himself for not printing a photo of Mick Guerra's mugshot. At the very least, he could have asked the clerk if he recognized the man.

"You think this Mick Guerra guy is staying here?"

Beanie said, "His parole officer heard he might be here."

"Sounds about right." The clerk rubbed his patchy beard. "We get a lot of ex-cons. What does he look like?"

As best as he could, summoning an image of Guerra's mugshot in his mind, Beanie described the man.

"I may have seen a guy who looks like that," said the clerk.

"Did you happen to see him on New Year's Eve?" asked Beanie.

"Can't say that I did," said the clerk, glancing at the stained tiles above him again, as though he might find the answers in the faded water rings. "Then again, I was focused on other events happening which were very odd."

"What do you mean?"

The clerk propped an elbow on the chipped Formica counter and leaned forward. "So, sometime around three in the morning, two fancy cars drive into the parking lot."

"Fancy cars?" asked Beanie, figuring the man was about to tell him about Kenneth Moreaux and Saul Biaggio, a topic he'd planned to inquire about after his questions about Mick Guerra.

Nodding, the clerk said, "A Mercedes came first. Then not long after that a Rolls Royce. And I say it was odd because folks that drive those kind of cars don't frequent this establishment."

"Right," said Beanie.

The clerk went on. "Now, I didn't see who got out of the Mercedes. I think whoever it was had already got out of the car by the time I noticed it was in the parking lot. But I definitely saw who got out of the Rolls. Older man with a distinguished way about him, like a wealthy guy, with that kind of rich dude swagger."

"And the rich guy went into one of the rooms?"

"He knocked on the door. Somebody opened it, and then the rich guy went in," said the clerk. "I was being nosy so I checked my records for room fourteen—that's the room the rich guy went into—and it was some French-sounding last name. Started with an 'M', I think."

"Could it have been Moreaux?" asked Beanie.

"You know I think it was," said the clerk. "So, some time passes. And then two guys come out of room fourteen. It's night so I can't really see, but one of the guys looks like he'd had one too many, you know? Like he's stone-cold drunk. And the other guy is sort of dragging him to the Mercedes. The guy is out cold, so the guy leans him over the hood of the Mercedes, then opens the back door and then grabs the guy, and stuffs him into the backseat. At that time, I'm wondering what's going on, but it's New Year's so, maybe the guy got a little too excited. It's one of those holidays where people drink too much, right?"

"Exactly," said Beanie, somewhat distracted as he realized the man, Saul Biaggio, hadn't been drunk. He'd been stabbed. That was why he was unable to walk on his own. Mick Guerra had stabbed Saul in room fourteen, and then Kenneth Moreaux took him out to the Mercedes.

"So, the Mercedes drives away," said the motel clerk. "Then, not five or ten minutes later, a woman comes out of room fourteen. She walks to the Rolls Royce, jumps in, and drives away. Of course, I'm even more—"

"Just a second," Beanie interrupted. "You said a woman came out of the motel room?"

The clerk nodded. "She must have been in there with the two guys. White lady. Couldn't tell what color her hair was, but it was pulled back like how a teacher would wear their hair."

"Like in a bun?" asked Beanie.

"Right." The motel clerk said, "So, I'm think maybe the woman was the old rich guy's wife. Maybe his girlfriend. She came to get her husband's car. Maybe."

"Yeah," said Beanie. But he wasn't sure about the motel owner's assessment. He didn't think the woman with her hair in a bun was Tammy Biaggio. Because, first of all, interior cameras at the Biaggio home showed Tammy going to bed and staying there, unlike Saul who had left the house.

So, who was the woman with her hair in a bun?

Beanie didn't know, but he had to find her.

35

"Did I stab Saul or not?" demanded Kenneth Moreaux as he dropped down into his leather chair.

Clearing his throat, Beanie took a seat in the chair opposite the man's desk.

Following his conversation with the motel clerk, Beanie had decided it was time for another conversation with Moreaux. Despite the man's mood swings and blackouts, Beanie hoped to jog Moreaux's memory about the night Saul was stabbed.

"Well, I'm not sure," Beanie began.

"I thought you were supposed to find out," Moreaux said, scowling at him. "You were supposed to help me clear my name."

"Mr. Moreaux, do you know a man named Mick Guerra?"

"Mick Guerra?" Moreaux asked. "Name seems familiar."

"Why is his name familiar?" asked Beanie, wondering if Moreaux didn't remember hiring Guerra to kill Saul because of the brain trauma.

Closing his eyes, Moreaux shook his head. "I can't remember. Why are you asking me about this guy?"

Beanie sighed. "I think Mick Guerra may have stabbed Saul. And he might have killed Ivan Rublev, as well."

"Can't say I was sad to hear about Rublev's untimely demise," said

Moreaux. "He poisoned Saul's mind against me, you know? Shifty guy. He never liked me. Why do you think Mick Guerra killed him?"

"Ivan Rublev claimed that Mick Guerra stabbed Saul," said Beanie. "And the main reason I asked you about Guerra is because the man was at the motel where you and Saul met in the early morning of New Year's Day."

"I don't remember going to a motel in Little Turkey."

"But, your car was seen on the CCTV camera and the car's GPS traced you to that location, remember?"

Shaking his head, Moreaux asked, "So, some camera footage caught me at this motel?"

Beanie scratched his chin. "Actually, no."

"Then there's no proof I was at that motel," said Moreaux.

"But your car was there," said Beanie. "How did it get there if you didn't drive it to the motel?"

Leaning forward, Moreaux placed his elbows on his desk. "Okay, you said Rublev thought Mick Guerra stabbed Saul. That means I didn't do it. So, my name is cleared, right?"

"I'm not sure," Beanie said. "The evidence shows that you called Saul from the burner phone and lured him to the motel. I have a theory. I think maybe you hired Mick Guerra to kill Saul."

"Can you prove it?" asked Moreaux.

"Right now, no," admitted Beanie. "I was hoping to talk to Guerra, not that I think he'll snitch on you, but stranger things have happened. And I was hoping you would remember hiring Guerra. Paying the man to attack Saul."

"Look, I didn't hire Guerra to kill Saul, because I didn't want the man dead," said Moreaux, his voice rising in irritation. "If I wanted Saul dead, I would kill him myself. But, I didn't. I can tell you this, though."

"What's that?" asked Beanie, once again jarred by the man's wild mood swings.

"I know why Guerra's name seems familiar," said Moreaux. "He had beef with Saul."

"What kind of beef?" asked Beanie, skeptical of Moreaux's claim, which seemed to come suddenly, out of nowhere, at just the right moment, to deflect suspicion from himself.

"Guerra showed up at the Biaggio offices one time," said Moreaux. "I was still working there, obviously. He demanded to speak with Saul. The receptionist tried to run interference, but Guerra pushed her aside and barged into Saul's office. Me and Irving were right behind the guy. We hurry into Saul's office, and Guerra has him around the throat. He's accusing Saul of fooling around with his wife?"

"His wife?" Beanie frowned. "Guerra is married?"

Moreaux nodded. "Can't remember his wife's name. But, Guerra told Saul to stay away from his wife … or he would kill him."

36

"Good news," announced Fields after Beanie sat across from him at Dizzy Jenny's.

Earlier that morning, Beanie had gotten a text from Fields, inquiring about lunch. Always amenable to meeting with his friend, Beanie texted his acceptance, confirming a time and place.

"Do tell," said Beanie, curious about the officer's jovial mood. And eager for some positivity, considering his frustration concerning his search for Mick Guerra, and the woman with her hair in a bun. Without the ex-con's story, Beanie didn't want to write the next follow-up article, in which he planned to float his theory that Kenneth Moreaux and Mick Guerra had conspired to kill Saul Biaggio. He didn't expect Guerra to come clean with him. The ex-con would almost certainly deny any involvement in the Saul Biaggio stabbing. But in the interest of objective journalism, he wanted to give Guerra a chance to present his version of events.

"I don't have to meet Amber's father," said Fields, picking up the menu.

"So the guess who's coming to dinner is canceled?" asked Beanie, taking a sip of the complimentary water.

"Thank God!" exclaimed Fields, shaking his head.

"How did you get out of it?" asked Beanie, glancing at the menu.

"I didn't get out of it," said Fields. "Amber's father told her it wasn't a good idea."

"And she agreed?"

"Not exactly." Fields sighed. "But she decided not to push the issue."

"Well, it's probably for the best."

"Probably?" Fields scoffed. "It's absolutely for the best. Did I tell you my commanding officer found out that Amber and I are seeing each other?"

Shocked, Beanie asked, "How?"

Fields shrugged. "This is a small island. People talk. Somebody probably saw us."

"What did your C.O. say?"

"Same thing you did," said Fields. "He called me into his office. Asked me if I thought it was a good idea to date the daughter of a known cartel member."

"And you said?"

Exhaling, Fields said, "I told him that Amber and her father didn't have a great relationship. They'd only recently reconnected after her mom passed away, so her daughter could get to know her grandfather."

"Was he satisfied with that answer?"

"I'm not sure," said Fields. "He told me to be careful."

"I agree with that advice," said Beanie, perusing the menu again, focusing on the description of the marinated goat kabobs with mashed plantains.

"I know he means well," said Fields. "He's looking out for me, but …"

"But you're a grown man and you don't need your boss meddling in your love life?"

Fields' expression grew apprehensive. "No, I was going to say … I think he wants me to be careful because he's suspicious of Amber."

Beanie gaped at the officer. "Suspicious of Amber? Why would you think that?"

"His assistant told me," said Fields, his voice glum. "Apparently, he wonders what Amber sees in me. He thinks she might be working with her dad to force me into becoming a PC-5 mole."

Exhaling, Beanie said, "Listen, I worried about that, too—"

"You don't trust Amber?"

"No, that's not what I meant," said Beanie. "I didn't want Lime Shoes trying to recruit you."

"He never could," said Fields, his gaze stern.

"I know that," said Beanie. "And as crazy as this sounds, Lime Shoes has something in common with your C.O. I spoke to him recently and he's worried you'll use Amber to bring him down."

"I would never do that," insisted Fields.

"And Amber would never use you," said Beanie. "So your C.O. doesn't have to worry and neither does Lime Shoes. Still, your relationship is going to make some people doubtful and suspicious."

"Look, I really like Amber," said Fields. "And I don't care what people think. I'm not going to let the doubts and suspicions ruin our chance for a future together."

Beanie sighed. "I know that, but—"

"I don't want to talk about this anymore," grumbled Fields. "Let's change the subject."

"To what?" asked Beanie.

"What I should have led with," said Fields, sheepish.

Confused, Beanie said, "What?"

"I was able to get some information about the Ivan Rublev murder," said Fields. "Apparently, fifteen minutes before you showed up at the Biaggio Loans office, a female housekeeping staff member entered the Biaggio offices at 7:23 pm and left at 7:46 pm. Now, this was odd because the cleaning crew had arrived at 5:05 pm and left the Biaggio office at 5:28 pm, then went on to clean the fourth floor, and left the building at 6:49 pm. That crew traveled to another office building."

"So, one of the housekeepers returned to the building? Why?"

"That's what Janvier wants to find out," said Fields. "But he can't find her and he needs to question her because Rublev was alive at 7:27 pm. His phone records indicate that he made a call at 7:27 p.m. to a restaurant to cancel a food order."

Beanie said, "Rublev was alive at 7:27. Then the housekeeper leaves at 7:46 pm."

"And you show up at 8:05 p.m. and find Rublev dead. No one entered or exited the Biaggio offices between 7:46 and 8:05 and there is only one way into and out of the office. No back door, or anything."

"You think the housekeeper killed Rublev?" asked Beanie, confused by the information, considering his theory that Mick Guerra had murdered Rublev.

Fields said, "Janvier hasn't said anything, but I think that's what he's thinking. And I think he might be right."

37

Beanie sipped his first cup of coffee of the day while reviewing the analytical metrics from his latest follow-up about the Biaggio case.

POLICE SEARCHING FOR POSSIBLE WITNESS IN LOAN EXECUTIVE MURDER had done well. The shares, views, likes, and comments were above par, much to Vivian's delight.

The information about the mystery housekeeper who had returned to the Biaggio Loans, Inc. office an hour after the office had been serviced turned out to be the impetus for most of the reader's comments. Most people believed the housekeeper had shot Ivan Rublev, or possibly had seen his killer. The reason behind the housekeeper's return to the office was highly suspicious to many readers, considering that, according to the police report, the owner of the maid service that cleaned the building stated there was no reason for one of his staff to go back.

Additionally, the owner stated that none of his employees would have been able to enter the office because they didn't have keys to any of the establishments.

"The building janitor lets my employees into the offices," said the owner. "When my housekeeping staff leaves an office, the door locks automatically behind them."

According to Fields, the janitor at the orange building confirmed that he had not opened the Biaggio Loans, Inc. offices for a housekeeper and video surveillance backed up his story.

Beanie stroked his chin.

If the housekeepers didn't have keys to the offices, then how had one of the housekeepers gotten into the office? Did the woman have a key? If so, how had she obtained it? She couldn't have stolen it from the janitor because he would have reported the theft to the police.

The desk phone interrupted his speculation.

"Roland Bean," he answered.

"I hope you're not busy," said Fields, a palpable excitement in his voice.

"What's going on?" asked Beanie, feeling his own anticipation ramping up as he wondered what Fields was about to tell him.

"Well, first of all, concerning Ivan Rublev," said Fields. "Janvier is still looking for the cleaning staff worker but enhanced still shots from the camera surveillance shows she has a weird tattoo on her hand."

"A tattoo?"

"Looks like that," said Fields. "Or maybe it's a burn. Birthmark, maybe. Or a scar."

"Interesting," said Beanie, feeling a spark of a memory of something he couldn't quite grasp.

"So, that's a lead," said Fields. "And moving on to the Saul Biaggio case, remember when we said Janvier should bring Mick Guerra in for questioning?" asked Fields.

"He's finally going to do it?"

"Only because the CSI guys found traces of Mick Guerra's DNA in Kenneth Moreaux's Mercedes," Fields said. "Initially, Janvier thought it belonged to a passenger in Moreaux's car, but Guerra has a criminal record, so Janvier wants to talk to him."

Beanie said, "My theory about Guerra working with Kenneth Moreaux makes sense now."

"What theory about Guerra working with Moreaux?"

"Didn't I tell you about it?"

"I don't think so," said Fields. "Why do you think they're working together?"

"I'd been trying to track down Guerra myself to ask him about Ivan Rublev," said Beanie. "I got in touch with his parole officer who told me he was staying at a motel in Little Turkey. I thought it could be the same motel where Moreaux and Saul Biaggio ended up on New Year's. So, I go to the motel and the clerk tells me he saw Moreaux and Saul arrive at the motel. I think Mick Guerra was in the motel room with Moreaux and Saul."

"And you think Guerra stabbed Saul?"

"I'm pretty sure he did," said Beanie. "Then Moreaux drove Saul to his rental house in Oyster Farms."

"Which is crazy," said Fields.

"But, Moreaux has been acting crazy since the accident," Beanie reminded him. "An interesting thing is that the clerk saw a woman arrive at the motel in a cab and drive away in Saul's Rolls Royce."

"Who was the woman?"

"Don't know," said Beanie. "But, she's got something to do with the attack on Saul because the used car lot owner got the Rolls from Mick Guerra."

"Which means the mystery woman gave Saul's car to Guerra," said Fields.

"Exactly," Beanie agreed, then asked, "Has Janvier had any luck finding Guerra?"

"Hasn't located him yet," said Fields. "He spoke to Guerra's wife but she claims she hasn't seen him since he got out of prison."

"Kenneth Moreaux told me Guerra was married," said Beanie. "He couldn't remember her name."

"Well, you'll never guess who she is," said Fields. "But you know her."

Confused, Beanie asked, "Who is she?"

"Lisette Javon."

38

"Lisette hasn't been in the office for the last few days," said the Biaggio Loans, Inc. receptionist. "She's been working from home."

Beanie stared at the receptionist, sitting across from him at one of the picnic tables beneath a tall palm tree in the culinary park, located on the northeast section of Pourciau Square.

After leaving the *Palmchat Gazette* offices with the intention of talking to Lisette Javon about her estranged husband Mick Guerra, Beanie headed to Pourciau Square where he spotted the receptionist getting a coffee from the Hullabaloo Coffee kiosk. He approached her, and she greeted him with a warm smile, agreeing to speak with him.

"Anyway, to answer your question," The receptionist continued, taking a quick sip of the iced chai latte she'd ordered. "I don't know much about Lisette's husband. I knew she was married, but I don't even know his name. She never talked about him at all. Quincy Irving told me her husband had been in prison but when I asked her, she told me it was none of my business, so I dropped it."

Nodding, Beanie asked, "Did the police ask you anything about the cleaning woman who was seen on surveillance camera entering the Biaggio offices before Ivan Rublev was killed?"

The receptionist said, "They asked me about the key to the offices.

They wanted to know if I had given the key to one of the housekeepers. I told them, no. Because I don't have a key to the offices. Only Saul, Ivan, Quincy, and Lisette had keys. Saul is in a coma. Quincy got fired and Lisette had the locks changed, just in case he'd secretly made an extra key. And Ivan is dead."

Beanie said, "So, really, only Lisette and the head janitor had keys to the office?"

The receptionist nodded. "And I talked to the janitor about it. He didn't give anyone a key because he doesn't have an individual key to our offices. He has a master key that opens all of the offices."

"Makes sense," said Beanie, scratching his cheek. "Then, only Lisette had a key to the office."

"Yeah," said the receptionist, shrugging. "But why would she give her key to some housekeeper?"

An hour later, back in his tiny cubicle at the *Palmchat Gazette*, Beanie continued to ponder The receptionist's question. Why would Lisette give her key to the mystery housekeeper?

Beanie wasn't sure she had.

He wasn't sure about anything except a strange, sinking feeling that Lisette Javon had something to do with the attack on Saul Biaggio. Which made no sense. Unless it made all the sense in the world. Beanie sighed. He needed to share his suspicions with his coworkers. Find out what Caleb and Stevie thought. Was he crazy? Or was his theory so crazy that it just might be true?

Fifteen minutes later, sitting in the breakroom with Caleb and Stevie, drinking his last cup of coffee of the day, Beanie said, "I found out today that Lisette Javon and Mick Guerra are married."

"Married?" Stevie gaped. "Are you serious?"

"Wait. Saul Biaggio's COO is married to the man who stole Saul's car, tried to extort Rublev, and may have been colluding with Kenneth Moreaux?" asked Caleb, his expression skeptical.

Beanie nodded. "And I know it's crazy but I'm wondering if she was in on the conspiracy."

Shaking his head, Stevie asked, "But why would she join forces with Moreaux to kill Saul?"

Caleb said, "Maybe she and Saul weren't as close as she led everyone to believe."

Beanie said, "Lisette did tell me that she didn't agree with Saul kicking Moreaux out of the company. But, I don't think she was so upset that she wanted to get rid of Saul. What I think is she may have gotten caught in the middle of her husband's scam with Moreaux."

"What do you mean?" asked Stevie.

"Her husband is an ex-con who needs money," said Beanie. "He might have agreed to kill Saul Biaggio for Moreaux. Lisette may have found out. Guerra might have threatened her. Told her to stay quiet, or else. I believe Guerra directed Lisette to drive Saul's Rolls Royce away from the motel. The clerk said he saw a woman in a bun. Lisette wears her hair that way."

Caleb said, "Okay what about the mystery housekeeper? You think Lisette gave the woman her key to get inside the Biaggio offices and shoot Ivan Rublev?"

Stevie said, "Because it's looking like the housekeeper might have had something to do with Ivan's murder."

Beanie exhaled. "The only other explanation is that Lisette Javon shot Ivan Rublev."

Caleb frowned. "You think so?"

"Fields told me an enhanced still image from a surveillance camera showed that the mystery housekeeper had a tattoo, or a scar on her hand," said Beanie. "I thought it sounded familiar and it's just occurred to me that Lisette Javon has a large, raspberry birthmark on her hand."

"It had to have been her," Stevie said. "But, do you really think she would shoot Ivan Rublev?"

Sighing, Beanie said, "She doesn't seem capable. I don't know."

Caleb said, "You know, housekeeping cleaning carts are pretty large. You think it's possible that Mick Guerra was hiding in the cleaning cart?"

"It's crazy, but I can see it," said Stevie. "Then it looks like housekeeping came back. You only see a woman on the camera. But inside the office, Guerra jumps out of the cart, shoots Rublev, then gets back into the cart and the cleaning lady leaves."

"It's crazy, but it makes sense," said Beanie. "Lisette must have found out that Rublev had evidence to prove Guerra had stabbed Saul. So, Guerra forced Lisette to help him get rid of Rublev."

"It might have happened like that," Caleb agreed. "But how are you going to prove it?"

Beanie said, "I've got to talk to Lisette Javon."

39

Staring at the spray of water gushing from the hose onto the hibiscus bushes near the porch, Beanie ruminated on the theory he'd developed with the help of his coworkers.

After spending the rest of the afternoon unsuccessfully trying to contact Lisette Javon, Beanie left work, picked up the boys from Noelle's mom's house, then stopped at a favorite restaurant for takeout. With Ethan and Evan inside watching cartoons, Beanie decided to water the flowers Noelle had planted several weekends ago.

Yardwork always helped him think.

And the more Beanie thought about it, the more he believed that Lisette Javon had been an unwilling pawn in the schemes of Kenneth Moreaux and Mick Guerra. Caught between a madman and her ex-con husband, the Biaggio Loans, Inc. COO probably thought she had no choice but to go along with the diabolical plan.

Guerra was a car thief, but if he'd agreed to kill Saul, Lisette had probably been too afraid to go to the police. Often, people didn't understand why witnesses stayed quiet but over the years, Beanie had learned that intimidation and coercion was a powerful thing.

Lisette hadn't answered his calls, texts, or emails, which was worrying, but tomorrow was another day.

First thing in the morning, he planned to—

"The bushes are looking good!"

Recognizing the voice of his neighbor, Anthony Mendez, Beanie took a deep breath and then turned toward the older man. As usual, Mendez was dressed in pastels, like an island sugar baron out for an evening on his yacht.

"Yeah, I'm trying to make sure they stay that way," said Beanie.

"Listen, I don't want to keep you," began Mendez. "But, you remember I told you about my friend who has a surveillance system like mine who lives on Porpoise Circle, across the cul-de-sac from Moreaux's rental house?"

Nodding, Beanie said, "You thought he might have some video footage from New Year's Eve."

"Yesterday," continued Mendez, "he calls to tell me he was reviewing his footage from New Year's Eve, which he hadn't looked at until now, and he thinks he recognizes Saul Biaggio on the surveillance footage."

"Where is the footage?" asked Beanie. "Did your friend give it to the police?"

"Not yet," said Mendez. "He's not sure what to do. He's the type who doesn't want to get involved. Afraid the cops will find a way to lock him up for something he didn't do. One of those people who believes that no good deed goes unpunished, and—"

"Would I be able to see the footage?" asked Beanie, anxious to get Mendez back on track.

"Oh, yeah. That's what I wanted to ask you," Mendez said. "You want to take a look? I told my friend to email the file. When you're finished watering your bushes—"

"How about we take a look now?" Beanie suggested.

An hour or so later, after he'd reviewed the surveillance video several times on the desktop computer in Mendez's office, which had been converted from a bedroom, Beanie rubbed his chin.

Standing behind him, Mendez asked, "What do you think? Should we call the cops?"

Trying to push past his shock, Beanie nodded. "I'll call a friend of mine on the force. His name is Officer Damon Fields. In the meantime,

I'll email myself a copy of the surveillance footage so I can show him when we meet up."

Mendez said, "I'm glad I showed it to you. I'm going to call my friend and let him know what's happening."

Minutes later, Beanie left Mendez's home and headed down the sidewalk back to his place.

His mind swirled with images from the surveillance footage. Video evidence he could hardly believe and probably never would have expected—or suspected.

The video showed a black Mercedes driving around the cul-de-sac and stopping in front of Moreaux's rental house. Next, a man exited the car. Standing near the car's hood, he pulled an object from his pocket, which turned out to be a phone. He made a call, pacing the length of the car as he talked. At one point, the man looked toward the camera.

Beanie recognized the man.

Mick Guerra.

After ending his call, Guerra hurried to the rear of the Mercedes and opened it. He reached inside and, seconds later, pulled a man from the backseat.

The man, who was clearly hurt, his shirt stained with something dark, stumbled, facing the camera.

Beanie immediately recognized the man …

It was Saul Biaggio.

40

After sharing the bombshell revelations from the video surveillance with Noelle, and following a quick phone call to Vivian, who wanted him to reach out to Mick Guerra again, Beanie decided on a trip to Guerra's apartment.

He wasn't expecting the ex-con to be around, and if he was, he didn't think Guerra would talk to him, but Beanie had to try. But he didn't plan to confront the man alone. He texted Fields, who was on patrol but promised to meet him at Guerra's address.

Ten minutes after leaving Oyster Farms, Beanie exited the coastal highway and made the turn on the road leading into Little Turkey. The impoverished neighborhood suffered from crumbling infrastructure and island blight, but its residents were known to stage protests and riots, demanding the better quality of life they deserved, even if they didn't get it.

Fifteen minutes later, Beanie pulled into the complex, a dilapidated collection of two-story units that had seen better days. He pulled into an empty parking slot near Guerra's apartment, then cut the engine and pulled out his phone. He texted Fields.

Dropping the phone into the drink holder, Beanie gripped the wheel.

The motel clerk had seen Saul Biaggio being dragged out to the Mercedes, clearly incapacitated. Beanie had assumed Moreaux had put Saul in the Mercedes, but based on the camera footage, Mick Guerra had gotten out of the car when it parked in front of Moreaux's rental house.

Guerra had removed Saul from the car and dragged him around the side of the house and into the backyard. Then Guerra returned to the Mercedes and drove away. Moreaux wasn't on the camera footage. He hadn't been with Guerra when Saul was taken to the rental house on Porpoise Circle. So, where had Moreaux been when Guerra was driving to Oyster Farms? Back at the motel?

An odd thought struck Beanie.

What if Moreaux had never gone to the motel?

After all, the motel clerk hadn't seen who'd driven up in the Mercedes and gotten out. What if Guerra had been driving the black Mercedes? Maybe Moreaux told Guerra to drive his Mercedes to meet Saul at the motel? Was it possible? If Moreaux called Saul and set up the meeting at the motel, then when Saul showed up, if he saw Moreaux's black Mercedes in the parking lot, he would obviously think Moreaux was in the motel room.

Beanie took a breath and checked his phone.

He frowned.

Fields hadn't texted back yet. Where was he? Beanie drummed his fingers against the steering wheel. Common sense told him to wait for Fields. But what if the officer had been called to an incident? Fields might not be able to make it. Beanie checked his phone again. Still no text from Fields.

Ten minutes later, Beanie made up his mind that he wasn't going to wait.

He didn't expect Guerra to open the door, but on the off chance that he did, Beanie wanted to question the man. See if he could get Guerra to spill secrets.

At the apartment door, Beanie knocked against the weather-beaten wood. No answer. After a minute or so, he knocked again, harder this time. Still no answer. He decided to walk around to the back of the apartment, where there was a small patio. Against his better judgment, he hopped over the waist-high railing and walked to the sliding glass doors. Cupping his hands against the glass, Beanie peered inside.

The small studio apartment was dim and gloomy. Beanie could just make out a couch against one wall and across from it a full-sized bed. Beyond that, a tiny galley kitchen, and—

A jolt passed through Beanie.

On the floor in the kitchen, in front of the stove, was the body of a man. Sprawled out on the light-colored tile, he was face down. A small pool of something dark spread from beneath him, creeping toward the chipped grout.

"Oh my God …" whispered Beanie, grabbing the latch. He yanked it. The door slid back. Beanie rushed inside and hurried to the man and dropped to one knee next to him. Carefully, he turned the man onto his back. It was Mick Guerra. Blood covered the T-shirt he wore.

Was he dead?

Beanie reached a hand toward the man's neck, to check for a pulse, and—

A low moan stole his attention. Beanie stood, listening. Where had the sound come from? Inching toward the living area, Beanie heard the sound again. Seemed to be coming from the bed. Only there was no one lying on it. A few more cautious steps alongside the foot of the bed, and then he saw it.

Or, rather, her …

Lisette Javon.

Lying on the floor on the opposite side of the bed. Beanie hurried to the woman. After calling her name, he helped her up, glancing at the plum-colored bruises on her pale skin.

"What happened?" asked Beanie, allowing Lisette to lean against his forearm and steady herself. As he guided Lisette to the couch and helped her sit down, Beanie's mind swam with confusion. The bruises on Lisette's face and the blood covering Mick Guerra threw Beanie for a loop. What could have happened between them?

"Lisette …" Beanie sat next to the woman. "Can you tell me what happened?"

Staring at Beanie, trembling, her eyes wide and haunted, Lisette asked, "Is he dead?"

Nodding, Beanie said, "I think so …"

A sob escaped Lisette's lips. "Oh my God … I didn't mean it, I didn't want …"

"You didn't mean what?" asked Beanie, though he had an idea.

"He attacked me …" Lisette cried, wiping her damp cheeks with trembling fingers. "He was so angry. I had to shoot him … he was going to kill me …"

"Why did he try to kill you?"

"Because I know the truth," gasped Lisette. "I was going to tell the police what he did."

"What do you mean?"

"Mick tried to kill Saul," said Lisette. "He told me to stay quiet about what he'd done, but I couldn't. So, I came here to try to persuade him to come clean, and …"

As patiently as possible, Beanie said, "Tell me what happened …"

Lisette released a deep shuddering breath. "It was after the New Year's Eve party. I didn't know it at the time, but Mick was there. Somehow, he crashed it. Sneaked into the ballroom. Once the party was over, he came to my apartment and forced his way inside. He forced me to go to this crappy, little motel where he had rented a room. He made me call Saul and tell him that I needed to see him. It was important. He told me to say, Mick is here and he's threatening me. Saul immediately came to the motel. Mick was lying in wait. He attacked Saul and stabbed him. Then he put Saul in the back of the car. And he forced me to drive Saul's Rolls Royce back to his house."

"Why didn't you tell the police sooner?" asked Beanie.

"I wanted to," said Lisette, shaking her head, tears streaming down her cheeks. "But, Mick said he would kill me, and after what he did to

Saul, I believed him. And he told me I had no proof of what he'd done."

"Why did Mick stab Saul?" asked Beanie.

"Because Kenneth Moreaux paid him to do it," cried Lisette, dropping her face in her hands.

"Are you serious?"

Raising her head, Lisette sighed. "You remember I told you that Mr. Moreaux wasn't as bad off as Saul thought?"

"You told me Moreaux was going to talk to some doctors at the Rakestraw-Blake Center," said Beanie.

Lisette nodded. "Well, I found out that Moreaux did see those neuroscientists. And they were able to help him. Moreaux has been faking his brain trauma."

"Faking the brain trauma? Why?"

"My guess is that Moreaux created a Plan B for himself, just in case Mick got caught and decided to snitch on him," said Lisette. "Moreaux planned to plead insanity and get off while Mick went back to jail."

Beanie asked, "So, if Moreaux didn't lure Saul to the motel, then how did his Mercedes get there?"

Lisette looked away for a moment, then back to Beanie. "I'm not sure about that. I think Mick stole Moreaux's Mercedes and drove it to the motel."

"Why would he do that?"

"Mick probably wanted to leave behind some evidence that would incriminate Moreaux," said Lisette. "Mick is not stupid. I think he figured Moreaux might betray him. So, he stole the Mercedes, put Saul in the backseat, and then drove Saul to Oyster Farms."

"Lisette—"

"We need to call the police now, don't you think?" asked Lisette, touching her neck, giving Beanie a view of the birthmark.

Recalling the gauze he'd seen on Lisette's hand, Beanie asked, "Did you hurt your hand? I seem to recall it was bandaged."

Lisette glanced at her birthmark, then at Beanie. "Bug bite. But it's fine now."

Beanie glanced at the raspberry birthmark again. He wasn't sure if her story about a bug bite was true, but he knew for certain she was the mystery housekeeper who'd entered the Biaggio Loans offices before he'd arrived. Beanie started to ask her about it, but the sight of her neck sparked a memory.

A photo of Lisette filtered into his head.

The photo Flo Taylor had shown him, from the Biaggio New Year's Eve party. Flo had thought Lisette's fake diamond pendant necklace was tacky. At the time, something about the necklace had seemed familiar to Beanie. Now he realized what it was …

He'd found a diamond pendant necklace in the grass in the backyard of Moreaux's rental house.

The diamond pendant necklace belonged to Lisette.

So, how had it gotten in the backyard?

Staring at Lisette, Beanie said, "I need to ask you something."

"Ask all you want, Mr. Bean, but my lovely wife will not tell you the truth …"

Beanie jumped at the raspy, sarcastic retort.

Lisette let out a yelp of surprise.

Several feet away, in the kitchen, Mick Guerra grunted as he struggled to raise up and prop himself against the lower cabinets.

Sweating and panting, Guerra said, "Lissy's little fairytale is an absolute lie …"

41

"You can't believe a word he says," said Lisette, scowling at her estranged husband. "He's a homicidal sociopath. They never should have let him out of Tiverton. But he's going right back to prison once I tell the police—"

"More of your lies," wheezed Guerra. "You really are a piece of work. Lying to the reporter. Telling him that I forced you to lure Saul Biaggio into an ambush when you know very well that—"

"Shut up, Michael!" commanded Lisette, jumping to her feet.

"I think the reporter deserves to know the truth," said Guerra.

"I told him the truth," said Lisette, grounding the words through clenched teeth.

"You told him a twisted version of it," said Guerra. "But you left out the part about everything being your idea."

"Lisette's idea?" asked Beanie.

"You can't believe anything Michael tells you," said Lisette. "He's a pathological liar!"

"The truth is that I wanted money and Lissy wanted to take control of Saul's company so she could use it to launder money for the Russian mob," said Guerra, pressing a hand against the wound in his abdomen.

Beanie gaped at the man. "What?"

Guerra grunted, "Lissy is the money launderer. Not Quincy Irving. But, that's what she wanted Ivan Rublev to think."

"That's a lie!" shouted Lisette.

Continuing, Guerra said, "And Ivan Rublev was fooled, for a while. Rublev convinced Saul to fire Quincy Irving. Once Irving was out of the way, Lissy had to get rid of Saul. So she cooked up this plan. You see, I haven't always been a loving husband to my deceitful wife."

"You've never been a loving husband," Lisette snapped.

"Saul knew that I wasn't very nice to Lissy," said Guerra. "She was able to use that to her advantage. She called Saul and told him I had kidnapped her, took her to a rundown motel in Little Turkey, and was threatening to kill her. Lissy knew Saul would come running."

"I told you not to listen to him." Lisette stepped in front of Beanie and glared at him, as though she were a mother scolding a recalcitrant child. "He is a liar!"

Standing, Beanie stepped away from Lisette and glanced at Guerra.

"Now, while Lissy was calling Saul and pretending to be scared for her life," said Guerra, "I was putting my skills to use at Kenneth Moreaux's house."

"Putting your skills to use?" asked Beanie. "You stole Moreaux's Mercedes?"

Coughing, the ex-con said, "Lissy told me to do that. She said we were going to blame everything on Moreaux because the man doesn't have the brains God gave a goat since his accident. Lissy used Moreaux's trauma from the accident to her advantage. She knew that Moreaux had pretty much lost his mind. Everyone knew the man was violent and had blackouts. Moreaux would be the perfect person to frame because he hated Saul."

"This is not true," disputed Lisette, sneering at her estranged husband.

Guerra said, "So, I steal Moreaux's Mercedes and drive it to the motel. Maybe twenty minutes later, Saul shows up. He knocks on the door, Lissy opens it, and I ambush Saul."

"And you stabbed Saul?" asked Beanie.

"With the knife Lissy gave me," said Guerra.

Beanie glanced at Lisette. "Kenneth Moreaux's knife. The knife he returned to Saul."

Shaking her head, Lisette said, "That's a ridiculous lie! There's no way I could have gotten that knife!"

"But, that's the knife Saul was stabbed with," said Beanie. "So, how could Mick have gotten it?"

Lisette paled. "How would I know? Michael must have stolen it, or—"

"I got it from you, Lissy," said Guerra, the exertion of his exclamation sending him into a fitting of coughing.

Beanie looked toward Lisette. "The receptionist said that you were at the office when Moreaux returned the knife. And you told her that you would make sure Saul got the knife back."

Blinking, Lisette hesitated, then said, "I gave that knife to Tammy. And that's who Mick must have got it from. He must have stolen the knife from Tammy, and—"

"You gave me that knife," growled Mick, his damp face drained of color. "You told me we needed it as part of the plan for Moreaux to take the fall for stabbing Saul."

"Is that true?" Beanie asked Lisette, suddenly considering the COO in a different light. A more diabolical light.

"Are you serious?" Lisette gaped, shaking her head. "You can't believe him! He is an ex-con. A criminal!"

"And she is a bitter, vengeful—"

"Shut up!" Lisette lunged toward Guerra.

Beanie stepped in front of the COO, stopping her progress. "Look, I texted a friend of mine, a St. Killian police officer. He's on his way. But, I think we need to call an ambulance—"

"I want to continue before you call," gasped Guerra. "Just in case I don't make it …"

Scoffing, Lisette said, "We should be so lucky."

Beanie glanced at the woman, disturbed by her flippant tone, and the menacing grimace marring her face.

The ex-con continued, "After I stabbed Saul, he stumbled toward Lissy and sort of fell on her. He reached out and grabbed at her. And she starts screaming that he snatched her necklace off. Some cheap fake diamond necklace. And she yells that we have to find it because it links her to the crime."

Beanie said, "But you didn't find it, did you? And you know why? Because it was dropped in the grass in Saul's backyard."

Mick laughed, then coughed. "Biaggio must have held that necklace in his clutches, then dropped it when I left him in the backyard at Moreaux's rental house. That was also Lissy's idea, by the way. She said doing that would help to make Moreaux look guilty. As would leaving the burner she'd used to call Saul in the Mercedes."

Beanie walked over to Guerra. "But I guess you didn't count on the cops finding your DNA in the Mercedes."

"No, I did not," said Guerra, grimacing. "But, somehow, I think that's what Lissy hoped would happen."

"My husband is telling you outrageous lies! I would never try to set up Kenneth for attempted murder," insisted Lisette. "I liked him! He was always nice to me!"

"Mr. Guerra, what about Ivan Rublev?" asked Beanie. "I saw you talking to him at Dizzy Jenny's."

Guerra shook his head. "I offered to tell him the truth behind Saul's stabbing and the reason why it happened. But, he didn't want to pay me."

"Rublev suspected you had stabbed Saul," said Beanie.

"Well, he was right about that," said Guerra. "He didn't know the whole story."

Beanie asked, "Did you kill Ivan Rublev?"

Guerra stared at him. "Lisette killed Ivan Rublev."

"That is not true!" Lisette screeched. "You can't listen to him!"

"I'd like to hear your husband's version of events," said Beanie.

Cursing, Lisette turned and stomped back to the couch. "He's only going to tell you lies."

Guerra said, "Lissy found out that Ivan had figured out that she was laundering money."

"That is so ridiculous!" Lisette seethed.

"How did he find that out?" Beanie asked.

Guerra said, "Some friend of his who worked at a bank in the Caymans where Lissy had opened a secret numbered account gave Rublev the information. Now, technically, banks don't violate client privacy but Rublev was able to convince the banker that Lissy was using that account for nefarious purposes. The bank didn't want the police to come after them, so the banker gave Lissy up."

Lisette shook her head, but Beanie believed Guerra. Rublev had told him about the Cayman banker he'd hoped would help him discover the identity of the money launderer. At the time, however, Rublev had thought the account belonged to Quincy Irving.

"Rublev confronted Lissy and told her he was going to tell the cops that she was a money launderer and I was the guy who'd stabbed Saul," said Guerra. "So, Lissy dressed up like a housekeeper, went to the office late at night, because she knew Rublev would be working late, and she shot him."

Cursing her estranged husband, Lisette sprang from the couch and rushed toward Guerra.

"Stop right there, wifey!" Guerra's harsh command was backed up with a gun, pointed at Lisette.

Shocked, Beanie took a step back, holding up his hands.

Lisette froze.

Grunting, Guerra used his legs to scoot himself to a sitting position as he trained the firearm at Lisette.

"I thought Lisette shot you," said Beanie.

"I did shoot him," said Lisette. "And then he wrestled the gun from me and knocked me in the head with it."

Chuckling, Guerra said, "Lisette is not exactly a good shot. Got me in the side, not the gut. Should have gone for the chest, or the head."

"Michael, please …" cried Lisette. "Don't shoot me …"

"Admit what you did," demanded Guerra. "Tell the truth. Tell this reporter that you planned Saul's attack."

Shaking her head, Lisette said, "I won't. I'm not going to lie—"

The gun went off.

Beanie dropped to the ground as Lisette screamed.

"You shot me!" Lisette gasped, pressing a hand against her arm. "You diabolical—"

"I shot you in the arm on purpose," said Guerra, his low tone like ice. "The next bullet will be between your evil eyes and I will not miss. Now, tell the truth, Lisette!"

Rolling onto his side, Beanie scrambled to his hands and knees, before slowly rising to his feet.

"Okay, fine …" Lisette shrugged. "I hired Michael to kill Saul and then help me frame Kenneth Moreaux for the murder so I could take over Biaggio Loans and continue laundering money for the Russian mob."

"What?" Beanie shook his head, staring at Saul's COO, shocked that she'd actually confessed.

"But, you lied to me," said Guerra. "You were never going to pay me."

"You were stupid to believe me," snarled Lisette. "Even if I did have money to give you, which I don't, I wouldn't. And I knew I didn't have to worry about you ratting on me because you'd be telling on yourself."

Guerra scoffed. "Somehow, when I vowed to be with you for better or for worse, I didn't realize I'd only get the worst of you, and never the best."

"You got the worst of me?" Lisette barked a mirthless laugh. "I got worse than the worst of you! I got a husband who didn't even know how to successfully steal cars and got caught and sent to prison!"

"Where you never visited me," said Guerra, a note of injury in his voice.

Lisette rolled her eyes. "Well, at least I sent money to your commissary account! I didn't let you starve in prison!"

"You should be the one in prison," accused Guerra. "Laundering money for the Russian mob! Plotting to kill a man who trusted you! Scheming to blame that murder on a feeble old man who's not in his right mind!"

Screaming and cursing, Lisette lunged at Guerra again.

Terrified that her estranged husband would blow her head off, Beanie grabbed her, trying to pull her out of harm's way, and—

The front door burst open.

"Freeze!" The command rang out as a dozen or so St. Killian police officers swarmed into the studio apartment. "No one move!"

"So is it true?" asked Stevie. "Saul Biaggio came out of the coma?"

Beanie nodded. He'd spoken with Officer Fields three days ago and gotten the news.

A few weeks had passed since the cops showed up at Mick Guerra's apartment. Both Guerra and Lisette had been arrested while Beanie was interrogated by Detective Janvier.

"Have you talked to Saul?" demanded Caleb, adding more sugar cubes to his tea.

"Not yet," said Beanie. "I hope to soon. But Fields said Janvier questioned him and Saul confirmed that Guerra stabbed him and Lisette was in on the plan. Guerra thought Saul was unconscious, but he wasn't. While Saul was on the floor in the motel room, bleeding, Lisette confirmed with Guerra that he was to drive Saul to Moreaux's rental house in Oyster Farms."

Caleb shook his head. "So, Lisette was money laundering."

Beanie said, "Ivan Rublev discovered it. Apparently, the police found a thumb drive in his pocket which outlined the evidence against Lisette. And they spoke to the Cayman banker who identified Lisette as the person with the numbered account where the dirty money was funneled."

"And Rublev was going to share that evidence with you," said Stevie. "But Lisette killed him."

Nodding, Beanie said, "Those enhanced camera surveillance shots that showed the birthmark on her hand pretty much prove she pretended to be the housekeeper. However, the gun that Guerra threatened to shoot her with was the gun Lisette used to kill Rublev."

"Crazy story," said Caleb, taking a sip of tea. "And how did she get involved with the Russian mob anyway?"

Beanie shrugged. "Not sure about that. Of course, Lisette is no longer talking. At her initial bail hearing, she entered a plea of not guilty."

"You think she'll beat the charges?" asked Stevie.

"There's plenty of evidence to tie Guerra to Saul's stabbing," said Beanie. "But, Lisette was pretty smart. Other than the fact that Moreaux gave her the knife that was used to stab Saul, there's really no physical evidence connecting her to Saul's stabbing. Still, there's evidence to tie her to Rublev's murder and to the money laundering."

"And she confessed her involvement to you," reminded Caleb.

"I gave my statement," said Beanie. "And I'll have to testify. Hopefully, it'll be enough to put Lisette behind bars with her husband. "

Caleb said, "Good thing is that Moreaux didn't stab Saul."

Beanie said, "He was glad to know that, but disappointed that Lisette tried to frame him by using his traumatic brain injury against him. He told me he was going to get some help, though. Hopefully the doctors at the Rakestraw-Blake Center will come up with a successful treatment plan."

Minutes later, back at his desk, Beanie reflected on Saul Biaggio.

He couldn't help feeling sorry for the man.

He couldn't imagine how betrayed Biaggio felt learning of his trusted COO's betrayal. Lisette Javon had convinced her estranged husband to kill her boss, a man Lisette had professed, it seemed to Beanie, genuine affection toward. Lisette had esteemed both Saul and Kenneth Moreaux as men she admired. Had it all been an act?

Beanie felt duped. Lisette had fooled him. He'd never suspected her. But why would he? It never occurred to him that she had motive, means, or an opportunity. Pondering it all now, in light of the recent events, Beanie supposed Lisette had lied about her feelings about Saul. She likely saw him as an easy mark. An old fool she could con while she stole his company and plotted his demise. Lisette was a heartless crook, determined to kill a man in order to perpetrate her twisted crimes.

Reflecting on Lisette and Mick, Beanie wasn't sure why they were estranged. They seemed made for each other. Two selfish, corrupt people, willing to murder a man and blame their crimes on an innocent victim. They were partners in crime.

The Caribbean Bonnie and Clyde.

Are you eagerly anticipating Beanie's next unexpected detour into a mystery waiting to be solved?

Then **Beanie's Mini Mystery Moments** are for you!

Get an exclusive quick-read mystery that spins off from one of Beanie's mystery adventures delivered straight to your email inbox!
https://BookHip.com/MZRMQQZ

ALSO BY RACHEL WOODS

SASSY SARCASTIC CAT COZY MYSTERIES

Sophie Carter, a struggling reporter for the *Palmchat Gazette*, teams up with a sassy talking Calico cat to solve crimes as she strives to become an influential investigative reporter

A SLY AND SINISTER TAIL

A COLD AND CALCULATING TAIL

A FOUL AND FRIGHTENING TAIL

A DARK AND DEVIOUS TAIL

REPORTER ROLAND BEAN COZY MYSTERIES

Roland "Beanie" Bean, husband and loving father, finds himself the unwitting participant in solving crimes as he seeks to make a name for himself as a reporter for the *Palmchat Gazette*.

HAPPY BIRTHDAY MURDER

EASTER EGG HUNT MURDER

MERRY CHRISTMAS MURDER

TRICK OR TREAT MURDER

GOBBLE GOBBLE MURDER

HAPPY 4TH OF JULY MURDER

SUMMER VACATION MURDER

HAPPY NEW YEAR MURDER

PALMCHAT ISLANDS MYSTERIES

Married journalists, Vivian and Leo, manage the island newspaper while solving crimes as they chase leads for their next story.

UNTIL DEATH DO US PART

NO ONE WILL FIND YOU

YOU WILL DIE FOR THIS

DON'T MAKE ME HURT YOU

THE PALMCHAT ISLANDS MYSTERIES BOX SET: BOOKS 1 - 4

RUTHLESS REVENGE ROMANCE SERIES

Gripping romantic suspense series with steamy romance, unpredictable plot twists and devastating consequences of deceit.

HER DEADLY MISTAKE

HER DEADLY DECEPTION

HER DEADLY THREAT

HER DEADLY BETRAYAL

MURDER IN PARADISE SERIES

A series of stand-alone women sleuth mysteries with murder, mayhem and a dash of romance, set against the backdrop of turquoise waters and swaying palm trees of the fictional Palmchat Islands.

THE UNWORTHY WIFE

THE SILENT ENEMY

THE PERFECT LIAR

ABOUT THE AUTHOR

Rachel Woods studied journalism and graduated from the University of Houston where she published articles in the Daily Cougar. She is a legal assistant by day and a freelance writer and blogger with a penchant for melodrama by night. Many of her stories take place on the islands, which she has visited around the world. Rachel resides in Houston, Texas with her three sock monkeys.

For more information:
www.therachelwoods.com
rachel@therachelwoods.com

facebook.com/therachelwoodsauthor
instagram.com/therachelwoodsauthor
bookbub.com/authors/rachel-woods
amazon.com/author/therachelwoods

ABOUT THE PUBLISHER

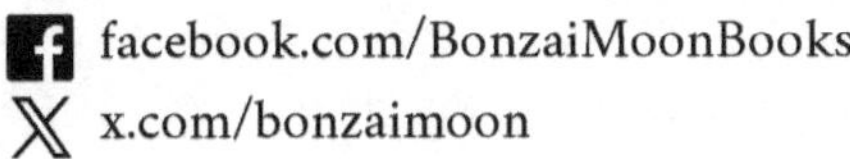

BonzaiMoon Books is a family-run, artisanal publishing company created in the summer of 2014. We publish works of fiction in various genres. Our passion and focus is working with authors who write the books you want to read, and giving those authors the opportunity to have more direct input in the publishing of their work.

For more information:
www.bonzaimoonbooks.com
info@bonzaimoonbooks.com

facebook.com/BonzaiMoonBooks
x.com/bonzaimoon